Away With Shadows

M.M. Skye

TAWCarlisle Publishing, LLC.

Contents

Away With Shadows

By M. M. Skye

Copyright

Chapter One

"IF SOMEONE ASKS ME one more time why I don't have a man, I'll pull one of their eyes out," Sharon Gable mumbled. Lately, most of her conversations had been about relationships. Particularly her relationships.

It was a beautiful and sunny day in downtown Columbia, SC, and Sharon stood at one of her big office window, looking out towards the street. She leaned closer, pressing her head against the windowpane, staring unabashedly when an elderly couple caught her attention. The gentleman got out of the car, walked to the passenger side, and opened the door. Not long after, the foot of a woman wearing low-heeled shoes appeared, planting itself onto the pavement. The gentleman took her hand and stood back as she rose from the seat of the car. Then, he removed her handbag from her shoulder and took a step back to close the door, still holding onto her hand. He pulled her to himself and kissed her gently on her lips. A smile came across Sharon's face as she watched the woman gaze into the man's eyes with love and affection. She daydreamed about having this kind of relationship someday.

Sharon looked up, caught part of her reflection in the window, and stepped back slightly so she could take in more of her own image. She wasn't bad looking. Some might even say she was beautiful. She stood five feet seven inches tall and had long, athletic legs and a small waistline. Today, she wore a dark-blue pencil skirt with a white and yellow short-sleeve blouse that buttoned up in the front. Her four-and-a-half-inch heels accented her calves. Her long, flowing hair was pinned to the left and rested on her shoulder. She wore brown reading glasses that perfectly complemented her caramel complexion and the shape of her round face. Her hazel eyes, rimmed with long lashes, made anyone who met her stop in their tracks just to look at her. Still, behind those sultry eyes laid a soul that was hurting and longing to be rescued from the pain and loneliness she felt inside.

Sharon closed her eyes to the hurt, tilted her head up to embrace the warmth of the sun shining on her face, and took in the glory of the morning. She gave thanks for all her blessings and tried to bury the fear of being alone for the rest of her life. It was one of the reasons she spent so much time at the office. If she couldn't be a success in her personal life, she certainly would be a success in her professional life.

At thirty-one years old, Sharon worked particularly hard alongside her partner to maintain the prestige and respect of their company. In the last five years, she and her partner had grown their interior design business to well over five and a half million dollars in revenue, and it was still growing. They experienced both the highs and lows of being successful women, especially as women of color, but they never let that dictate their success. People from the United States and Europe contracted with the pair.

Watching her parents work hard to provide for her taught her from an early age to not let societal stigmas stop her from accomplishing what she wanted to do in life. In addition, being an only child made her self-sufficient.

When she was eight years old, her parents died in a car crash, turning her life completely upside down. The police report showed the accident occurred when her father swerved to avoid hitting a deer while they were coming back from visiting his best friend and his family in Savannah.

A firm knock at the door interrupted her from her daydream. Sharon hadn't noticed her friend standing in the doorway of her office.

"Hello, are you still in the land of the living?" asked Kera. She leaned on the door post with her coffee mug in one hand and her purse in the other.

Sharon turned and replied, "Oh Kera, you scared me. I apologize. I was just watching this elderly couple out on the street. You should have seen them. They looked cute together."

Kera swiftly walked over to the window. "Are you sure it was the elderly couple you were watching or were you daydreaming about you know who?"

Kera Prescott was her best friend and co-owner of *Prescott Gable Interior Design, LLC*, which they'd run for the past ten years. It seemed only natural for the two women to go into business together after graduating with honors from the New York School of Interior Design.

Kera was a beautiful, slender-faced woman, with oval-shaped eyes. She wore her hair in a pixie cut style that complemented her high cheekbones and the dimple between her right cheek and upper lip. Unlike Sharon, Kera was an athlete at heart. She was the captain of her high school and college volleyball team. She was three inches taller than Sharon and curvy in the hips.

The two were nominated best looking and voted most likely to be successful. As young girls, they did everything together and were inseparable.

"What?" said Sharon. "No. Girl, you know me better than that."

"Okay. Then besides the older couple, what had you so deep in thought that you didn't answer my question," Kera asked.

"Question? What question are you talking about?" She was completely clueless.

Kera folded her arms and stared at Sharon with one eyebrow raised as she walked over to fill her cup from the Keurig machine.

"Look, if you think you're going to get out of this one, think again, missy. It has been three months since we've had any fun together, and this time, you're coming. No excuses."

"What is it this time?" Sharon sucked her teeth and rolled her eyes as she walked back to her seat.

Kera looked at her with empathy. "I just want you to have some fun for a change."

Sharon drew in a deep breath to say that she would give in to whatever event or trip her friend had planned for them, when she spotted the bright light reflecting off her friend's hand.

Kera held out her hand to show Sharon her engagement ring. Sharon could hardly contain her emotions. She placed her hands on her cheeks and yelled with joy. Both women jumped up and down together, screaming with excitement. It was difficult for either one of them to speak.

"Would you be my bridesmaid?" asked Kera.

"Yes, you know I will! First, I want to know when this happened, and why I'm just now seeing this!" She looked at the ring with extreme happiness for Kera as they sat on the sofa in her office.

Kera's smile was radiant. Sharon could tell she was overjoyed and waited patiently as her friend tried to gather her thoughts so she could tell her what took place.

"Do you remember when Gregg and I were invited to have dinner at his parents' last night for game night?" Sharon nodded in agreement.

Kera said, "Instead, we all met up for dinner downtown at California Dreaming, and once we finished dessert, a singer came out and sang *Sweet Lady*."

Sweet Lady was Kera and Sharon's favorite song when they were younger. They'd sing and sway to the beat of the song every time the DJ played it on the radio.

"I was so excited when I heard the music playing in the restaurant," Kera continued. "My legs became numb—so much so that if I stood up, I'd fall flat on the floor."

Sharon's mouth was open so wide, she could hardly speak. She scooted her hips to the edge of the cushion, trying hard not to show the real emotions she experienced inside. While she was completely happy for Kera, she couldn't help thinking about her own happiness. Everyone around her had found their true love.

"I don't know how my baby pulled it off, but he was able to get the singer to come to the restaurant and perform for me," Kera said. "The guy sounded so much like the original singer, I had to make sure it wasn't the real artist performing. If it had been, I would have been up there trying to sing with him. I wish you could have been there, Sharon. It was so beautiful. It almost felt like I was in a fairy tale, and I was the main character in the story."

Sharon could tell how disappointed Kera was that she hadn't been there to help her celebrate her engagement. There was no reason she could come up with to explain her absence, other than the truth.

"I just wanted to relax at home alone, without being interrogated by the family about why I don't have a man in my life, and why I'm not married yet," she said. "Those conversations get old after a while. But if I'd I known this would be one of the most important nights of your life, I never would have missed it. I sincerely apologize, and I hope you know I would never not be there for you."

"I know. So, tell me more of the glorious details!"

"Well, I was so distracted by the love song, I almost missed Gregg kneeling down in his Armani suit on the pocket square he pulled from his matching jacket. He surprised me with a poem expressing his love for me. I didn't think he knew anything about poetry. Shoot, I've never seen him read anything other than Business Weekly."

Sharon listened excitedly to the rest of Kera's story. Gregg had nervously stroked his beard several times as tears of joy slowly flowed down his face. He took several deep breaths, trying to make sure he didn't fumble through his proposal. Finally, he mustered up the courage to ask if she would marry him and become his forever lady.

"I couldn't hold back the tears of joy," Kera said. "This was the moment I'd waited for. I felt like the world around us seized in time when he gently took my hand and spoke those heartfelt words coming from the depths of his soul. It was like he knew deep down that as soon as he'd released them into the atmosphere, nothing could stand against us."

Sharon held Kera's hands as she listened attentively to her talk about the most exciting night of her life. This was her Cinderella story coming true. If she could only have some of the same happiness, it would be the most enthralling time of her life. Not a fairy tale she'd read in a book, but a real-life experience she could tell her friend.

Sharon placed her hand on her heart, unable to keep back her own tears of joy. She was both happy for her friend and also fearful that she would never have that kind of happiness in her life.

Ever since they were little girls, Kera had a list of what she wanted in a relationship. When Kera got hurt by her college boyfriend, she practiced celibacy, at least until Gregg came along. Although spiritually, she knew what they were doing was wrong, the temptation was too much for her to say no to his advances.

Kera held up her hand, flexing her fingers in and out to see how the ring looked against her skin. It was a 0.7 cut round Pave diamond engagement ring from Tiffany & Company.

"Girl, he went all out on this one."

"Gregg has great taste," said Sharon. "Oh, Kera! Had I known this would turn out to be the happiest moment of your life, I would have been there to help you celebrate. I apologize for not being there. When is the wedding?"

"In three weeks." Kera shrugged. "I know it seems sudden, but we didn't want to wait too long. In two months, Gregg is going away to Kentucky to help out with one of the branches there. He'll be there for twelve weeks. If we don't do the wedding now, we'll have to wait until he returns. We want to make it official as quickly as possible."

Sharon looked at her friend confidently. "It's a good thing you have the best designers and planners in town."

Kera's cheeks rose with happiness. She stretched out her arms and held onto her friend tightly, thanking her for her support.

"Hey, no need to thank me. You know I love you and Gregg," Sharon said.

Kera had met Gregg Wilson three years ago at a conference for professional business owners in Atlanta, Georgia. It was love at first sight. Sharon and Kera were talking to one of the guest speakers when he approached and said he wanted them to meet a special client of his.

Kera had immediately locked eyes with the six-foot, clean-shaven man. He sported a low haircut, which was neatly trimmed and lined to complement his face, and he was built like a stallion, ready to be driven to any destination Kera wanted. Sharon couldn't think of a more perfect match for her friend.

Gregg was in the banking industry and had recently been promoted to VP of operations at one of the largest banks in Atlanta. He accepted the offer two weeks ago to be transferred to the southeastern region, giving him the perfect opportunity to be closer to Kera. He took it as a sign from above that they were destined to be together.

"What is it you were insisting I attend earlier?" asked Sharon, just now remembering what had started the conversation.

"Oh yes, Gregg and I are having our engagement party at my house on Saturday. It's just a small group of friends and family, so I expect you to be there."

"This Saturday, as in tomorrow?" Sharon asked.

"Yes, and you have nothing to do, so I expect you there at three o'clock sharp." Sharon had known what her friend was about to say from the look on her face. Kera wasn't one of those people who had a filter on her tongue. She definitely inherited that from her Aunt Patsi, who said exactly what she meant. Sharon put up no fuss and agreed to come, despite the last-minute invitation.

Kera hugged her. "I'm heading out. I'll see you tomorrow, and please be on time." She picked up her purse, grabbed a few books from the coffee table, and started towards the door. "I have to pick up a few things before the store closes."

"So, you just came to drink my coffee and leave," said Sharon.

Kera laughed. "Yep, and I love you, girl… later." Before shutting the door, she quickly turned back with one of her biggest smiles. "Oh, before you go, I need to tell you we received a letter from an investor in Paris. He wants us to open a store there and would like to have a conference call with us this week to discuss the proposal. What do you think about that?"

"This is awesome! I'm so excited. It's finally happening." Sharon was hardly able to contain her emotions.

Kera looked at Sharon with excitement. "Girl, this is what we've been talking about all our lives. This could be a great opportunity for us to get international exposure." Kera sent her a sly look. "Also, if you go to open our office there, it may give you a chance to find love. Think international love… sounds romantic."

"Me? Girl, you know we work better together. Besides, love is the farthest thing from my mind these days."

"Well, it'll have to be you, because I'm about to be a happily married woman, and Gregg will just be starting his new position with the bank. We can't go abroad right now. You and I will always be in business together; that's not a debate. The business is named after both of us, after all. When Gregg and I need a break, we'll definitely call you up."

"Let's not jump ahead of ourselves," said Sharon. "We need to hear what they have to offer and take it from there. A change of scenery wouldn't be a bad idea though, seeing how the only pleasure I have going on in my life is work. Paris *could* be a relief from all the chaos."

"See? I told you. We'll talk later. In the meantime, I have to go. Love you, girl!"

"Love you too! Later!"

Sharon returned to her desk to finish some work before leaving the office for the day. She could only imagine the endless possibilities

Paris would offer her. She'd often dreamed of seeing some of the many attractions there. The food looked exquisite in some of the foreign films she watched with her parents on television. The very thought of those times spent snuggled between them made her think of her favorite ice cream, pralines and cream. Even now, she was tempted to swing by the store on the way home just for the sweet treat.

A feeling of loneliness crept into her spirit, and it frightened her. Knowing she would be going home to an empty house made her feel like an old woman. Sharon yearned deeply to be able to come home and share her day's experiences with the man in her life. Someone who would put his own concerns aside just to listen to hers. To have him look at her with such desire and fire in his eyes, would make all her worries go away. Sharon dreaded being home alone with the thoughts of her own lonely life ahead of her since her faith in love was fading away.

Chapter Two

SHARON ARRIVED HOME AND flopped down on the couch in the entertainment room to watch television. Instead of watching her favorite channel, Home and Garden, she searched for a movie. She came across a love story that immediately drew her interest.

If only love happened like that.

She thought back to the conversation she'd had with Kera earlier that day. After she'd left the office, Sharon couldn't help but admit to herself that her friend was right. She didn't have anything to do in her free time because her job had become her personal companion.

She missed having the company of a man. She wanted someone to tell her he couldn't make it through the day without talking to her, and she wanted to feel the warm embrace of his arms around her.

She needed to feel as though she were special and to know that she
wouldn't be taken advantage of.

Memories of her ex-boyfriend came to mind. For six years, she'd had
an on-again-off-again relationship with Mark Whitten: Mr. Wannabe
Casanova himself. It ad been almost five months since she called it off
with him. Mark was very handsome, measuring six feet two inches tall
and weighing two hundred and twenty-five pounds of pure muscle.

He was the sort of man who could talk his way into a woman's heart
within two minutes of speaking with her. Lord knows he worked his
way into hers. Mark was a successful owner of two restaurants, one
in Charlotte, NC, and the other in Columbia, SC. He had a house
in each location and would travel back and forth to keep up with the
demands of his businesses, among other things.

He wasn't a man who wanted to be tied down. Deep down, Sharon
was aware of this disheartening fact. Even knowing he wasn't the one
for her, like so many other women, she'd thought it would be better to
have a piece of a man than to have the courage to remain single while
she waited on the one designed for her.

Sharon was the type of woman who did everything to prove that
she could be a good helpmate for her man. Unfortunately, she ended
up handling all of the wifely duties without receiving a vow or commitment on his part. Towards the end, he'd made her feel as if their
relationship had plateaued to the lowest level. In fact, the only time
he acknowledged his feelings for her was when his friends expressed
how lucky he was to have her in his life. When they were both alone,
his display of love was limited to when he wanted to get her in bed.
The intimate parts of their relationship weren't enough to make him
be faithful to her at all. So instead of trusting that she deserved more,
she settled for someone who treated her like frequent hotel points you
get every time you check out.

She remembered when they made love. It was what she considered to be the best and felt that no other man could make her body move in such a sensual way. She couldn't help thinking about how he had pulled her close to him with anticipation of making love to her. Every time Mark touched her, he made parts of her body respond to him without hesitation. Slow and steady was his routine, but that didn't stop her blood from flowing at sixty miles a minute. It was a feeling that kept her coming back to him every time.

On their last night together, they'd just returned from dinner to his house on the lake. Sharon made up in her mind that she'd had enough and decided to break it off with him. She wanted more from a man and finally felt, after watching so much of her life become wasted in a relationship that was going nowhere, she deserved more. There was also the timely piece of information she received via email before their last encounter that helped reinforce her stance.

The more she thought about it, the more Sharon came to see that Mark had known he had a good thing with her and didn't want to give it up. She assumed, in his arrogance, he thought her "tantrum"—which was anytime she disagreed with him—was a result of her dislike of him traveling so much. It would be just like him to back off for the moment and let her have the time she needed to come to "her senses." It wasn't the first time they had gone through this.

"I understand that you miss me a lot," he told her, "and I'm sorry I'm not here for you as much as you need me to be. My business is booming, and I need to make sure things continue to go well for me... I mean for us. Just be patient with me, baby. I'll make it up to you. I promise."

She'd looked into his deep, dark eyes and felt as though she was a piece of Dove chocolate that would melt just from looking at him. He had a masculine voice that spoke to her soul. She thought, *Lord, if he doesn't step away from me, I'll do something I'll regret later...* Before she could complete her thought, he placed his thick lips against hers and kissed her with such passion, she couldn't resist kissing him back. With one hand on the small of her back and his other hand holding the back of her neck, he made sure to give her something to remember him by until he returned.

He was unaware that Sharon had received an anonymous email showing pictures of Mark in California with another woman. Come to find out, his business trips to Santa Barbara were to meet up with his ex-fiancée, who was now carrying their child. This affair had been going on for the last year and a half of their relationship.

Sharon had been devastated and instantly angered by the information, and she'd vowed to never let another man play her like The Gap Band in a concert ever again. The soul tie she felt with him was strong, and she had to do everything she could to release herself from him.

She looked at him with fury and said, "I can't do this anymore, Mark."

He pulled back slightly from her. She saw the realization in his eyes that she was indeed serious about what she said to him. She was sure he hadn't expected to ever hear those words coming from her. Not after all this time together. A look of confusion came over his features. He was probably thinking that a man in his position was entitled to not have this sort of thing happen to him.

She waited for him to say something that would change her mind, but he remained silent. He couldn't think of anything that would make the conversation they were about to have any easier.

"I don't know what you mean. What's going on with you, honey? You've been acting like something is pressing heavily on that beautiful brain of yours since I got here. I have just what you need. Come on and let's do what we do best and send daddy on his business trip with something extra to think about on the plane. We have about two hours before I have to leave to go to the airport." Mark smiled with a devilish grin. He just knew he had her in his power again.

"I'm not doing this anymore with you. We're done here. It's over. That's what is going on. I'm no longer going to play second fiddle to your instrument. Goodbye, Mark, and tell Trish I said she can have you. I can't believe I let you use me like that." He stood, looking bewildered.

"Baby, I can..." Sharon cut him off in mid-sentence.

"Save it for her or the other women you may have been with besides me. All these years, you knew that having a family was very important to me, and yet you strung me along, knowing you were making a family with someone else. Such a fool I've been. I knew in my heart that you were being unfaithful to me, but I held onto a fantasy that you would settle down with me." She gazed up at him with great sadness and pain in her eyes.

Mark reached out before letting his hand fall to his sides. "How can I make you realize how much you need me? There are more important things between us than these silly notions of calling it quits."

It wouldn't work in his favor. She'd had enough and was glad for the courage to finally end the relationship.

"You know I don't blame you; I blame myself," Sharon said. "I lowered my standards and settled for a man who isn't even worth the socks he's wearing. You disgust me, but I still wish you well." Sharon gave Mark his key, turned, and walked towards the door. Mark tried his best to convince her to stay, but she wasn't hearing anything other than the door as she slammed it shut behind her. She walked out of his home and vowed to never go back to him again.

Chapter Three

It was three o'clock in the morning, and Sharon tossed and turned in her sleep, troubled by the same recurring dream of the night the accident killed her parents. The screeching of tires sounded on the darkened road, and the smell of gas fumes permeated the atmosphere. Impossibly long seconds passed by once the wheels left the pavement, where no further sound could be heard in the stillness of that dreadful night. And then suddenly, a small whimper broke through the silence. A faint cry to the parents who were no more could be heard from the backseat of the car.

"Mommy, Daddy, where are we?" cried the little girl.

The more she called out to them, the more exhausted she became. No response came, and the situation grew grim.

In her dream, Sharon became both observer and child. She wondered what happened. She remembered little of what could have transpired minutes before the crash, just a loud noise which sounded like thunderous lightning hitting the ground.

In the distance, she heard sirens blasting in the air. Her body was tightly fitted in her booster seat, unable to move. The front seat was pinned against the backseat. Her little hand reached out to touch her mother's soft hair. Her father was slumped over the steering wheel. There was barely any sign of life in either of their bodies. She felt alone and scared. Tears formed in her little eyes.

Then suddenly, she saw a figure of a woman who spoke to her in a still, calm voice.

"Help is coming, honey. Just hold on and listen to my voice," she said. Then the woman prayed, asking for protection over the little girl and her parents.

The little girl and the woman waited for what seemed like hours for help to come. Once the ambulance and the fire department arrived, they rescued the girl from the mangled car. She was assessed and taken to Children's Hospital nearby. As she listened to the voices surrounding her, fear and anxiety flooded her at the same time. She had been diagnosed with a concussion but suffered no broken bones.

"This little one was protected by something or someone," exclaimed a man's voice "There's no way she should have survived that crash. Absolutely no way!"

Once the voices were no longer in the room, Sharon opened her eyes to see the woman she had seen the night of the accident standing near her.

"You're going to make it, honey, she said. "You're going to grow up and become a successful woman. The love that was put inside you, make sure you use it to show others that love is powerful and can change any negative situation. Hold onto it. There will come a time when you'll have to rely on it to give you strength. Believe in yourself and never let anyone tell you that you can't make it." Then, the woman left the room.

Neither young Sharon nor grown-up Sharon had any idea who the woman was, but it was the last time either of them would see or hear from her again.

It'd been twenty-nine years since her parents' death, and she could still hear the voice of that woman speaking those words just as clearly as she did then.

Sharon sat up in bed. Feelings of loss intensified as she dealt with the lingering effects of the dream. She remembered that a week after the accident, when she was released from the hospital, Kera's parents took her home to live with them. Neither of her parents had siblings. Her father's parents had died when he was in his teen, and her mother's parents had died in a house fire when she was in college. So, she had no one but her best friend and her family.

She knew her parents loved her, and they had provided her with the best that life had to offer.

With tears streaming down her face, Sharon couldn't help but let out a loud cry. She opened the nightstand drawer beside her bed and pulled out a photo of herself and her parents on the day of her ballet recital. The photo was taken two weeks before the accident.

Glancing back at the drawer, she caught sight of something. She reached in and pulled out a card her dad had given her on her fifth birthday. On the card, he wrote the words, "Baby girl, when you need help in this world, the answers to all life's mysteries can be found inside of you. If you listen very carefully, there's a small inner voice within that will guide you. Always remember that no matter what, my love for you will never end."

A fresh set of tears welled up in her eyes, along with a slight smile. She clutched the card to her chest, cried, and prayed—something she hadn't done in such a long time. She gave thanks for how far she had come since the accident. Then, she drifted off to asleep again.

The phone rang at around seven thirty the next morning. Sharon was sleeping so peacefully, she didn't acknowledge the ringing. Having not gotten a full seven to eight hours of rest, she enjoyed this moment of tranquility.

Sharon lay there until nine o'clock. Then, feeling refreshed in her mind and body, she rose to take a shower, but before she could get one leg out of bed, someone buzzed her from her front gate.

She walked to her bedroom window and parted the sheer curtains to see who it was. It was Kera. Sharon pressed the button to open the gate, and Kera drove up to the long driveway, which curved to make coming and going easy. She parked by the entrance that led to the kitchen and got out with what Sharon could only guess by the packaging was breakfast she picked up for them from Chick-fil-A.

Sharon lived in a secluded neighborhood outside the city. Her home was almost thirty-five hundred square feet and had four bedrooms, with a large open floor plan that offered easy access to every inch of her home. Though the home itself was made with modern, clean lines using a lot of glass and brick, the art on the walls, rugs, pillows, and everything else she used to decorate her home gave it a barn-style rustic look. She had scoured all of the antique shops within a hundred miles of her home for just the right items to fill her house.

She was extremely fond of her outdoor garden, with its manicured lawn and custom-tiled infinity pool, which was right off the lake. The lake could be seen through the windowed French doors inside her family room.

Sharon enjoyed drinking her morning coffee on the outdoor veranda and watching the sun come up over the serene waters of the lake in the calm air. Being close to the water made her feel serene and peaceful and far away from all the noise in the city. That was just how she wanted it.

She grabbed her robe, put on her slippers, and headed out of the bedroom to see what her friend wanted. By the time she made it down the stairs, Kera had already used the spare key to enter the house and make them some coffee.

"What are you doing up so early?" said Sharon. "Are you okay? It isn't like you to get up early, especially on the weekend."

"I was so excited about the engagement party, I had to drive over to tell you what I think could be good news for you," Kera said as she fixed them coffee. Sharon noticed how extremely happy she was.

"Okay, spill it."

"What do you mean?"

Sharon pushed one side of her mouth up and gave her a look as if to say *I know you're up to something*.

"So, let me hear it," Sharon said.

Kera took a deep breath and said, "Well, I wanted to tell you that Gregg's best man is in town, and he's *fine*. I mean really handsome. I really think you should meet him."

Sharon stopped her friend before she went any further with the conversation. "Kera, I love you, but I'm not ready to meet anyone."

Kera interjected, "Well, you need to. Now don't get me wrong, you're like a sister to me, and you're too beautiful and talented not to have a man. I want you to have your Boaz like I do."

"Girl, please, Boaz." She chuckled with amusement. "Everybody can't be Ruth, and I don't need another man thinking he can play with my emotions."

Kera stirred two spoonsful of sugar and toasted marshmallow mocha creamer into her coffee and took a sip. She looked at Sharon and said, "All I know is... he's tall and handsome, with the most beautiful eyes I've ever seen on a man. He has a great occupation, and he's highly recommended by Gregg. I've met him several times, and he's down to earth. A no-nonsense type of guy with no player labels on his resume. You'll see what I'm talking about when you meet him today."

"So, what is his great occupation?"

"Gregg says he's a successful engineer from California who moved back here to help out his father's company."

Sharon asked, "Really? So, he's from South Carolina?"

"I thought you weren't interested in anyone," Kera said.

"I'm not!" exclaimed Sharon. "I'm just curious, since you said he relocated back here."

"Hmm, okay," mumbled Kera, with a smile on her face

"Can't a girl ask questions? He probably has a girlfriend somewhere, and I'm not going through that again." Quickly dismissing the memory of how Mark had made a complete fool of her during their relationship, Sharon couldn't help being curious about this mystery man her friend was hyping up to her. Sharon didn't want to let it be known that she was interested in a relationship again, even though she felt lonely.

Chapter Four

It was almost time for the engagement party. Sharon laid out a pink strapless sundress and her wedge-heeled sandals. It was too hot for her to wear her hair down, even though they would be by the pool. She decided to wear a loose ponytail and put on some eyeliner, mascara, and natural-colored lip gloss. She chose sterling silver waterfall earrings and slim silver bangle bracelets to match her dress.

Sharon had just enough time to take a shower and get dressed before heading over to Kera's. It took her about forty minutes to put her clothes on and head out the door. Just before leaving, she went into one of her guest rooms, picked up the gifts she had bought for the soon-to-be-married couple a few days ago, and packed them into her luxury car. It would take her thirty-five minutes to drive to the other side of town, as long as traffic wasn't backed up.

When Sharon arrived at Kera's, she noted by the amount of cars on the street and in the driveway that the crowd was more than a small group of friends and family, as her friend had said. Sharon wasn't sure if she could handle the pressure if most of the people there had dates.

Once inside, Sharon pulled Kera away and complained, "I thought you told me this was a small gathering, and I see people here with dates."

Kera explained that most of the people who had come were Gregg's colleagues from work, and they weren't couples, but they all knew each other.

"My mom and sisters are here in the kitchen, so you don't have a thing to worry about," Kera continued. "Oh, just so you know, Aunt Patsi is here also. You know she has had her fill of what she calls *happy relations in a glass.*"

They were on their way to the kitchen when the doorbell rang.

Kera told Sharon, "Go in. I'll be in there in just a few minutes. Let me see who's at the door."

Sharon acted as if she would continue on but turned back to see Kera scurry towards the door. She watched as Gregg shook hands with a person obscured by one of the columns holding up the arch separating the entry from the rest of the house. A big smile came across Kera's face as she greeted him as well.

She overheard Kera say, "Hi, Bradley. It's so nice to see you again." She was about to lean out further to catch sight of the man when someone passing to her right bumped her. She mumbled a hasty apology and went towards the kitchen to bide her time and get her nerves under control.

***

Gregg looked back at Kera as she greeted his friend. He saw the glint in her eye. The glint that said she was making plans. Even without the sparkle, he could tell by the tone in her voice what she was up to.

He quickly disengaged his fiancée's hand from his best friend's and placed an arm around his shoulder as he led him down the hall and into the living room.

Gregg introduced Bradley to his family and to his other friends who had flown in two days earlier. Most of them he knew, but there were a few, mostly like invited by Kera's parents, that he'd never seen. If this party was any indication of the wedding events to come, things were quickly getting out of control. That thought led him back to his soon-to-be-wife and the havoc she was trying to reap.

He led Bradley to the buffet laid out on long tables in the backyard near the grill. He promised to return before his friend finished his food, then went back into the house to find Kera.

He caught sight of her serving one of the elderly women her mother served with in church and waited patiently for her to finish before excusing them.

"Baby, would you please come here for a minute?" he said in a quiet tone that belied his irritation.

"Sure, honey, I'm coming."

Kera answered him innocently and obediently followed him, but he wouldn't be deterred from telling her to mind her business and not try to play matchmaker.

They slipped away into one of the guest bedrooms. For most of the people there, they had grown accustomed to the two disappearing for a while. It was no surprise to them what they were doing either.

"I know you want Sharon to be happy but let it happen naturally like how we met." He carefully brushed back the lone curl touching her left eyebrow. "I don't want you to be disappointed if they don't hit it off. Please promise me you'll let them come together on their own terms."

She replied in a soft, concerned voice, "You're right, baby. I just want her to be happy. She hasn't been herself these past few months since what's his name showed his natural…"

Gregg bent down to kiss her, so she wouldn't complete her sentence, and she seemed to welcome his kiss. His woman wasn't slow. He knew she was aware of his affectionate manipulation, but she wasn't complaining—she enjoyed every minute of it.

She broke contact just enough to say, "We have guests, honey."

He didn't care. At that very moment, he wanted her. One of the many characteristics he loved about her was that she had a heart for others. It was alluring. He knew that if she put her heart out there for others as she often did, she'd be the perfect mate for him. Making her his wife and mother of his children wasn't a question.

He reached back to close the door, stood in front of Kera, and lifted her up onto the king-sized bed. He kissed her passionately and pulled back her hair so he could feel the entire shape of her face. As he beheld her, he knew his love for her was revealed in his eyes. Gregg found it impossible to keep his emotions under control.

He whispered softly in her ear, "Kera, I can't wait until we become Mr. and Mrs. Gregg Wilson. I want to make love to you every night without hesitation. Baby, the way I feel, right now, at this very moment, I want to fill you up with so much of me, I feel I'm about to burst."

Kera kept her eyes on his as she gently guided him closer to her so that he had no choice but to accept her invitation. Their love for each other was undeniably contagious. He figured that everyone around them could feel the vibrations of their heartbeats when each entered a room.

"Baby, this is where you belong," Kera whispered softly in his ear. "I'm going to make you the happiest man alive. I can't think of any other man I would have as my husband," He closed his eyes, kissed her, and made love to her as if they were the only two people in the world.

***

All the women were enjoying themselves in the kitchen as they laughed, talked, and prepared the food. Kera's Aunt Patsi, who Sharon considered her own aunt, was almost three sheets to the wind from drinking too many of the orange cardamom bellinis that Kera's oldest sister had made.

"So, Sharon, how have you been?" asked Patsi.

"I've been good, Aunt Patsi. Business is going well for us," she added, as an explanation.

"So, when are you going to get a man, honey? You're too pretty to be without one. I'm going to search out one of those young tenders out there, and I bet I won't leave this party without one." Patsi burst into a loud laugh.

The air got really thick around Sharon with Patsi's question. She really didn't know what to say. She didn't want to tell Aunt Patsi to mind her business or tell her that her behavior was the reason her relationships didn't last longer than they did.

Respectfully, she stated, "I'm waiting on God to bless me with the right one."

Patsi looked straight at her and said, "Honey, you aren't getting any younger. Get you a man."

Patsi was Kera's youngest aunt, and she was, shall we say... very confident in her beauty. She was in her late fifties but had the body of a thirty-year-old. She worked out several times a week and was a vegan by choice, but her favorite drink was anything with alcohol. She wasn't a typical aunt—the kind who would show a girl how to be a young lady. Her way was to do whatever you wanted in the moment and worry about the consequences later. Patsi's sister Sara, on the other hand, was quite the opposite, which would often cause a strain between the two.

Patsi had been married several times, and each of her former spouses had been wealthy men. She said they were what she preferred. Unfortunately, she could never hold onto them. Kera said her fear was that they would leave her for other women. So, she would drive them away, never knowing if they would love her even in her old age. On occasion, Sharon had heard her voice what seemed to be her motto. "Get them before they got you, so you don't have to feel the hurt and shame of being rejected."

Her last marriage ended after only three years. Despite her insecurities, her image was what she worked so hard to maintain.

Sara looked at her sister as if she could cut her lips off with just the roll of her eyes.

Sara screamed, "Patsi, please put the glass down! Don't pay her any attention, Sharon. Her liver is acting up and causing her to talk that nonsense."

Patsi quickly retorted, "I know exactly what I'm saying, and you may want to listen to Aunt Patsi, honey. I can teach you young girls a thing or two." She raised her glass in the air, then took a gulp of wine.

Minutes later, Kera walked into the kitchen and noticed that the atmosphere was a little strange, so she turned up her lips and commented, "Auntie Patsi, what are you talking about that has the whole kitchen giving you the stink eye?" Everyone laughed. Patsi just lifted her glass in salute before continuing to take a drink.

"Sharon, may I borrow you for a minute?" asked Kera.

"Sure, what's going on?" replied Sharon.

***

"Bradley, where are you, man?" Gregg asked.

Bradley barely registered his friend's voice, let alone the question. The woman who walked in next to Kera had taken almost all his attention, along with his breath. Bradley immediately took notice of her. All conversations ceased around him as he took in each of her features, including her hair and face, then getting momentarily stuck on her lips. Those lips. He. imagined what it would be like to feel her lips against his. He could take hours getting to know those lips.

"Yeah, man, I can get some of that," Bradley said.

"What?" whispered Gregg in Bradley's ear. "Are you all right, man? You seem a million miles away?"

"Of course, man... I'm all right. I was..." Bradley stumbled over his words, trying to gather his thoughts as he watched the most beautiful woman he had ever laid eyes on follow his best friend's fiancée from across the room. He knew he had met some amazing, talented, and attractive women, but that woman was stunning.

"Man, who is that woman next to your fiancée?"

"Her name is Sharon." Gregg smiled and gave a chuckle. "She's Kera's best friend and business partner."

"Follow me so we can talk. Right now, you look like you need some fresh air or to mop up some of the drool on the side of your mouth," Gregg said jokingly.

Bradley reluctantly followed Gregg through a door on the opposite side of the room that led back into the backyard, listening intently as his friend filled him in on Sharon.

Unfortunately, one of Gregg's fraternity brothers interrupted him, whom he'd only been introduced to a few minutes before but could tell from his mannerisms what type of character he was.

Clinton Payne stood by the grill, trying to let every woman present know that he was on the hunt for his next victim. Clint, as he said he preferred to be called, was known as "the life of the party." Gregg had said that most of the people there knew what kind of person he was and tried hard to ignore him. Even though he had a lot stacked against him as a gentleman, Gregg said he regarded him as one of his best friends. Not only had they graduated from college together, but they were also from the same hometown. In the brief background Gregg had given him about Clint, Bradley learned that he came from a broken home and had to care for his family all on his own.

***

Having moved through the living room and spoken with what seemed like every one of Kera and Gregg's friends, Sharon allowed Kera to lead her out to the pool, where some of their old friends were hanging out near the barbeque grill. Kera's father, Samuel, wore his *Back up. Grill Master at Work* apron. Sharon talked to him for a little bit. She felt comfortable with Samuel and almost wished she could remain by his side for the rest of the party. He was genuinely interested in how she and Kera were doing in their business. Not to mention, he loved her like a daughter. Taking her first relaxing breaths, she gave courteous nods and short greetings to some of the people who walked up to Samuel for different cuts of meat.

While Kera spoke to one of their colleagues, Sharon noticed Samuel wiping his head, then looked around to see if he had anything cold to drink within arm's reach. Seeing nothing, she asked, "Do you want me to get you something cold to drink from the kitchen?"

The relief on his face at her offer almost made her feel guilty for silently hoping he might decline her invitation so she could remain with him.

"That would be wonderful. Sara told me she would get me something a while ago, but she must have gotten distracted."

Sharon flashed him a knowing smile then headed for the kitchen. As she walked up the steps to the house, she caught sight of who she could only guess was Bradley, since she hadn't gotten a good look at him in the entry hall, standing across the lawn talking to Gregg and a few of his friends.

Sharon was so taken by his appearance that she didn't look down to see the disturbed rug she was about to trip over. She was able to catch her fall by grabbing the side table by the door as her right foot got entangled into the thread of the oriental rug. She played it cool until she was inside the house, then looked out the corner of her eye to make sure no one saw her embarrassing moment.

Thank God, he didn't see me.

A little smile appeared on her face.

It had been a long time since she was instantly attracted to someone.

Chapter Five

After delivering Samuel's drink to him, Sharon walked over to Kera. "Who's that guy over there?" asked Sharon, pretending she had no clue who the gorgeous guy was standing next to Gregg. She took a thorough scan of his stunning frame. A pleasant charge went through her as she watched him from across the way.

"Who's who?" asked Kera.

"The one who is standing to left of Gregg."

"Oh, that's Bradley. Bradley DuPont. Gregg's best man." Kera turned slightly away from Sharon so it was hard for her to make out the expression on her friend's face.

"He's available and very prosperous," Kera said, giving Sharon a side glance.

"Bradley is thirty-six years old," Kera began. But Sharon couldn't help filling in some specifics for herself as she stared at him. He was six feet-five inches tall, and his stature was that of a basketball player. He had a dark complexion and perfectly round eyes with curly lashes, and his lips were sculpted with such precision, only the Good Master himself could have done it.

"Bradley is the second child of three boys born to Mr. and Mrs. DuPont. Gregg told me that his father had been the director of research for Savannah River Site, and his mother had been a teacher in the local school system.

"His mother passed away from lung cancer when he was in high school, and it took a toll on the family. Ironically, she never smoked a day in her life. Gregg said she was one of the most caring mothers in the world. She attended all their school functions and even cheered her sons on in their sports activities. Bradley received a scholarship to the University of Sacramento for both his academic merits and his athleticism. Gregg said that out of the brothers, Bradley was most like their mother, sharing her heart of gold. They had a really close relationship."

At this point, Sharon wondered if Kera wasn't putting extra on her description of Bradley. He almost sounded too good to be true.

"He also left behind some painful memories from his time in Sacramento. I don't know what happened to him there. Gregg wouldn't go into detail."

This, more than some of the other details, intrigued Sharon.

Kera trailed off for a moment before taking a deep breath and continuing.

"Charles, who is two years older than Bradley, is a well-established prosecuting attorney. He played professional football for almost three years until a knee injury ended his career. Gregg says he looks just like his good-looking father. Ladies love him, and he knows how to play his cards to get them." Kera's voice dropped for a moment as she tried to mimic Gregg.

From what I hear, he's the type that feels the whole world owes him something and acts like he was God's gift to everyone he meets. He was very jealous of Bradley, and he made it his business to let his brother know it every time they were around each other. Can you believe that? I think Charles has a lot of demons he's dealing with and doesn't seem to care about how his actions affect others. Greg said he has one weakness, but he wouldn't tell me her name. It seems he's hated himself for allowing the one person who loved him most to get away from him."

Sharon looked at Kera.

"What?" Kera said, looking back at her and pausing in her diatribe.

"I just wonder how you keep all this information straight in your head."

Kera seemed to think about it for a moment then shrugged. "It's interesting," she said before moving on.

"As for the youngest of the three, Ken is a combination of both his brothers. He's two years younger than Bradley and was a straight A student in school. He was voted most likely to succeed and was very good at track and field. He was also well known in the streets as a person not to cross. Ken was the exact replica of his mother, in complexion and physical features.

Ken was accepted to some of the most prestigious schools: Yale, Florida A&M, Harvard, Howard, and Cornell University by the time he was seventeen years old. When his mother passed away from cancer, and his father followed her soon after from a massive heart attack, he didn't care about any of it. He got in trouble with the law for everything from drinking and driving to getting into bar fights. Gregg said he was on a path of destruction for a while."

Sara and Samuel walked out on the patio, interrupting Kera, and she turned with everyone else when they tapped their glasses to get everyone's attention. Kera's mom asked for her daughter and future son-in-law to stand by her and her husband, so she could give her speech of wisdom to the couple.

With tears in her eyes, she said, "Thank you all for coming to celebrate this joyous occasion with us, as we prepare to unite my middle daughter Kera and my soon-to-be son-in-law Gregg in matrimony. Gregg, you're like the son we never had. I'm so grateful for you coming into our family and giving it some balance. Now my husband won't have to feel like he's the only man in the world among all these beautiful women. I've always wanted my daughters to have the kind of love I have with their father. We've been happily married for over forty years, and we're still as passionate about each other as the day we met."

Aunt Patsi blurted out, "Make sure you love her good, Gregg." She gave him a look that said *you know exactly what I mean.*

"Don't have my niece walking around here like a prune, son. She has too much to put on a shelf. Look at me!" she exclaimed. Glancing over the patio, she winked at Gregg's frat brother Clinton. Sara looked around at her spirited sister and rolled her eyes in frustration.

***

Bradley watched as Clinton raised his glass to her. He knew full well Clinton didn't see Patsi as anything more than a sugar momma. He followed Clinton's gaze as it slid to Sharon. Bradley clenched his fists and was close enough to overhear Clinton whisper to one of the guys that he would make his move on her.

Bradley smirked to himself. *That would never happen.* She didn't look like the type who would fall for Clinton. Besides, Bradley had his own agenda for her, and as soon as he could, he would make his move to get to know her.

After the toast was over, he watched as Clinton slithered over to Sharon. He didn't know what Clinton said but judging from Sharon's reaction, it wasn't welcoming.

Sharon gave Clinton a look that Bradley could read from where he stood. It said... *Back up, jerk.*

"Sharon!" Clinton called out loud enough for everyone within a few yards to hear. He licked his lips as if he had barbeque sauce dripping from his mouth. He moved closer to her as if he wanted to eat her up and spoke to her in a low voice that Bradley just barely caught as he sidled up to Sharon's other side. "I would love to get to know more about you, lady."

Bradley saw Sharon open her mouth and decided to interrupt before things got ugly. "Hey, baby, you're low on your drink. Shall we get you another glass?"

***

Sharon turned to follow the deep voice, only to look up and see Bradley. She couldn't say anything. Her throat felt as if it was swelling. The touch of his hand in hers sent a message straight to her innermost part, and she couldn't feel her legs. She only managed to say, "Yes, please."

She was happy to get away from Clinton, and even happier when she walked to the bar with Bradley. Just looking up at this tall stallion, smelling of Giorgio Armani cologne, had her on the edge. She tried so hard to keep it together, but her thoughts about him were racing.

When he looked into her eyes, somehow she could tell their thoughts were in sync.

"Thank you for rescuing me from Clinton," she said.

"It was my pleasure," replied Bradley, looking into her eyes as if he could see into her deepest thoughts.

She held out her hand to shake his. "I'm Sharon."

Looking at her with a slight smile that said exactly what he wanted to say, he replied, "I know who you are."

Sharon looked at him with curiosity. "Really? How's that?"

"I inquired about you earlier, and Gregg told me a little about you."

A feeling of unease came over her. *I hope he didn't tell him everything. He doesn't need to know everything, especially about my messed-up personal life.*

"So, how about that drink you were getting me?" asked Sharon. She didn't know what to say to him; what she wanted to do was somehow disappear from the party without being seen. She feared something else would happen, like him asking too many of the wrong questions about her past relationship.

He reached over to get her a fresh glass of Moet & Chandon Imperial. "So, tell me, how do you know the happy couple?" he asked as he handed her the glass.

"Kera and I have been friends for most of our lives, and we run an interior design business together. I was there when she met Gregg. I'm both friend and family." She looked over in the direction of Kera and Gregg. Watching them together brought so much joy to her.

"They make the perfect couple, don't they?" he asked.

"Yes."

He looked at her and asked, "I'm not trying to pry, but I noticed you're not wearing a wedding band or engagement ring; is there any reason why?"

Quickly turning her head towards him in a sarcastic position, she said, "You just jumped right in there, huh?"

With a clever grin, he answered, "Life's too short to waste time. So, I don't."

She thought, *Here we go again. I'm not falling for this. I don't care how fine he is—and good God, he's fine. God, your creation of man is beyond my imagination because you chiseled him out of the finest clay.*

She imagined him with his shirt off, and, judging by the size of his arms, she knew he was in shape. The way he looked in his Army-green jeans and matching fitted tee made her mind go into some places it hadn't been in a while. She snapped back from her thoughts to make sure he didn't notice how she was staring at his physique. She had no rebuttal to what he had said and nodded in agreement and took a sip from her glass.

She noticed Bradley look around them. "Would you mind us going somewhere a little more quiet so we can get to know each other?"

Sharon looked around, catching a few envious looks on some of the other women's faces and a satisfied smile on Kera's lips and readily agreed. "Yes, sure."

Bradley pointed to a bench by a big tree, and she nodded, more than ready to move out from under everyone's scrutiny.

Bradley led Sharon away from the crowd and waited for her to sit before taking a seat at a comfortable distance from her. *She could really like this man.*

They talked for what seemed like only a few minutes about her and Kera's relationship, upbringing and business, but it must have been much longer since her drink cup was completely empty and had been the last time she tipped it up, only to come away with a few drops of liquid.

"Can I get you another?"

She was about to reply when Bradley's phone rang. He looked down at the display, frowning, "Excuse me, Sharon. I need to take this call." He looked at her with regret and a little agitation.

"Of course. Go ahead."

He stood and took a few steps away. "Hello?" He paused, obviously listening to the person on the other line. "What? I'm on my way." Bradley turned back towards her, his eyes frantic. He walked back over to her and held her hand to apologize. He stopped midsentence and leaned down to kiss her cheek. "I've really enjoyed talking to you, but I have an emergency. I would like to see you again soon. Could I get your number from Gregg?"

Sharon nodded and wondered what kind of emergency would have him in a near panic.

"Is everything okay?"

"I hope it will be," he said before letting her hand go and walking swiftly back towards the house.

When Kera and Gregg caught sight of how fast Bradley was moving through the house, Gregg ran after him to find out if everything was all right,

"Bradley, man. Are you okay? I saw you and Sharon talking outside for a while. Is everything all good?"

When Bradley glanced back at him, he was relieved. "I was coming in to look for you to say good night. I just got a call from my grandfa-ther's nurse. He had a heart attack. He's being taken by ambulance to the hospital now. I'm going to meet them there."

"Wait." Gregg took hold of Bradley's arm when his friend made a move to keep walking. "Do you want me to go with you?"

"No, man. This is your engagement party."

"And? The guests will still be here when I return," Gregg replied right before Kera and Sharon walked up.

"What's going on?" Kera asked, looking back and forth between them.

Gregg glanced at Bradley, silently getting permission to share what was going on. After a nod from his friend, he filled the women in. "Bradley's grandfather had a heart attack, and I'll be going with him to the hospital."

"Oh no, is he okay?" Sharon asked.

Gregg watched as concern shadowed her features and knew that the two had already started to form a connection.

Bradley cleared his throat. "From what Linda, his nurse, said, it was a bad one. The EMTs seemed reluctant to give her hope that he would pull through."

Gregg watched as Kera and Sharon glanced at each other. "We'll come, too," said Kera.

Before anyone could make another move, Kera walked down the hall to where her parents were speaking to an older couple who had just put on their coats and explained the situation loud enough for him to hear. She then asked her parents to request that the guests stay and continue with the party; she and Gregg would return as soon as they could.

Chapter Six

Bradley paced the Heritage Medical Center hallway, talking to someone on the phone. From what Sharon saw and heard, he seemed to be arguing with the person on the other end of the line, and it didn't sound too good.

"Are you coming or not, Charles?" he asked angrily. He had been waiting for almost an hour, and there was no news of his grandfather's condition yet. "I've been trying to contact Ken, but I can't get an answer. I'll keep trying to reach him, and I ask that you do the same. Hurry up and get here, please!" Bradley took the phone away from his ear and touched his thumb to the display before slipping the phone into his pocket.

From where the three stood, they could see doctors, nurses, and lots of medical equipment going in and out of the room.

Gregg walked over to Bradley, giving him a one-arm hug while taking Bradley's free hand with his other. "I'm here for you, my friend."

"We're praying for you and your grandfather," said Kera. She placed her hand on Bradley's shoulder briefly.

Sharon stood against the wall, watching, not knowing what to say to Bradley. She saw how much pain he was in and wanted to tell him that she understood. It had been so long since she had been to a hospital. She knew all too well about pain and loss since her parents passed away. She found herself more concerned for Bradley and what he was dealing with than she expected. She wanted to hold him in her arms and tell him she would be there if he needed her, but she didn't want to come off as being too forward. She barely knew this man.

As if he could sense her thoughts, Bradley looked up to catch Sharon's stare. With a slight smile and overbright eyes, he returned her stare.

Not wanting to seem insensitive, Sharon walked over and touched his arm. As much as she could guess, they had a mutual attraction for one another, but in the silence that passed between them, she was surprised to see more in his eyes. Bradley turned and embraced her as naturally as if they had known each other for a long time, hugging her tight without quickly letting her go. It was as if the feeling of her body next to his gave him comfort, and she would allow him this moment of peace.

Suddenly, the door to his grandfather's hospital room opened, getting everyone's attention. They all turned to face the doctor as he came out.

He approached Bradley, "We did all we could for Mr. DuPont. Now it's just a matter of time." He put his hand on Bradley's shoulder. "I'll be praying for your strength in the Lord."

"Can I see my grandfather now?" Bradley asked.

"Sure, take all the time you need."

Gregg walked over to Bradley, not knowing what to say to his friend. He only knew that he had to be there for him whenever he needed a shoulder to lean on. The pair of them had been through some good times and had seen each other through some bad ones too. Facing him, Gregg gave him a reassuring nod. "We'll be in the waiting room when you come out."

"Thanks, man. I really appreciate that,"

As Bradley walked towards the outer doors of the ICU, he looked at Sharon. "Come with me?" he asked, holding out his hand.

She glanced over at Gregg and Kera as a feeling of discomfort fell into her soul. She wondered why he had asked her to go into the room with him and not Gregg. After all, Gregg was his best friend. Besides, she'd just met him and certainly didn't know his grandfather. She looked back at Bradley, who watched her with tears in his eyes.

"Please."

Sharon didn't want to say no. She remembered how Kera and her family were there for her when she experienced her loss. Making up her mind, she gently put her hand in his and followed him through the doors.

As they walked up to his grandfather's hospital room, she squeezed Bradley's hand. Fear and trembling came over her. She flashed back to when her father was lying in his hospital bed, tubes running in and out of him, with machines doing most of the work of keeping him alive. Her mom had succumbed to her injuries shortly before the paramedics arrived. She hated that she never got to say goodbye.

Sharon stopped at the sliding glass door to give Bradley some time to spend with his grandfather alone and watched the interaction between the two.

When Bradley came closer to his grandfather's bedside, he noticed that his eyes were closed as if he were sleeping. He paused for a moment to allow time for him to remember the times he and Gramps would spend long nights talking about how precious life is. The memories only left Bradley feeling more vulnerable and dejected.

Bradley leaned over and whispered, "Gramps. Gramps. It's me, Bradley."

His grandfather slowly opened his eyes, allowing time for his vision to become clear enough to see his grandson's face.

"Son, you're every bit of your father?" his grandfather spoke in a weakened voice.

Bradley smiled, trying to hold back a new set of tears. His grandfather looked at him and put his hand up to touch his face.

"Don't worry about me, son. God has been good to me. I've lived a wonderful life. I'm ready to go home. I can't wait to see your grannie, your mom, and your dad. Seventy-eight years in this land is a long time. I want you to live your life and not worry about me." He took a deep breath. "Have you heard from your brothers?"

"I talked to Charles a little while ago; he said he was coming, but I can't get in touch with Ken. I left him messages."

Bradley turned to look at Sharon just to make sure she was okay. She gave him a nod and smiled.

"Well, you know your brothers," said Gramps. "They haven't been right since your parents' deaths. Continue to be patient with them. They love you; they just don't know how to show it. If you'll admit it, deep down inside, you love them too," he told him.

"I'll try my best, Gramps," Bradley said.

"I know, son... I know."

His grandfather tilted his head, sniffed as if he smelled an unfamiliar scent and asked Bradley, "What is that lovely fragrance? I can tell there's a woman present." He gave a weak chuckle as he spoke.

Bradley beckoned for Sharon to come through the sliding door so his grandfather could see her. She walked up to the bed and stood beside Bradley.

"Gramps, this is Sharon," Bradley said proudly.

Sharon gave his grandfather a small smile and greeted him politely, looking nervous.

"Oh, my goodness. Hello there, young lady, and where did you come from?" A big smile came across Gramps' face. "You're a sight for an old man's sore eyes on his death bed." His voice weakened with each breath he took as he struggled to speak. Sharon's smile grew, but she still looked a little shy from where Bradley stood.

"You don't have to be afraid, honey. I don't bite." His grandfather paused for a moment before speaking again. "Sharon, did you know that your name means you can bring love and a new start to life? I can see that in your eyes."

Sharon looked at his grandfather, who didn't talk like a man who had had a heart attack at all. He had full capacity of his thoughts and his sense of humor. When Sharon gave him a big smile, he gave her one back.

"I know you'll make my grandson happy," Gramps said. "He's a terrific person, and I'm not just saying that because he's related to me. We DuPonts are strong, hardworking men, and we take care of our own."

He watched as Sharon opened and closed her mouth a couple of times with a frown on her face. He was about to interrupt when his grandfather's machine made a loud, continuous beeping noise.

All of the sudden, the older man's breathing became even more shallow. Bradley stepped forward even as he noticed Sharon stepping back, then freezing.

Bradley pushed the button beside the hospital bed to call the nurse.

"It's okay. Sssh. Don't push it," Bradley whispered to his grandfather, trying to keep the panic out of his voice.

His grandfather continued to struggle, seeming almost desperate to get his next words out. "You're the glue, Bradley. You keep your brothers together."

"Okay, Gramps. Just..." Bradley tried to soothe him again, but he wasn't having it.

"My papers." He heaved. "Papers in my office desk... important."

"Sure. Sure. Take it easy, Gramps." *Where were those nurses?*

"Love you, son." His grandfather breathed out more than spoke, his intense gaze deepening even further with his inhale, then softening with his next exhale before his eyes glazed over and went still.

The buzz in the room went chaotic as the nurses filed in, pushing him and Sharon back through the sliding glass door so they could work on reviving his grandfather, but Bradley knew he had just heard his old man's last words, and it gutted him.

Eventually, the nurses and doctors filed out with the head nurse offering her condolences and allowing him a few minutes alone with his grandfather's body.

With tears blurring his vision, Bradley stepped up to the bedside of the man who had sacrificed everything for him and his brothers and taught him how to be a man of integrity. He kissed his grandfather on the forehead and sobbed. At one point, he felt Sharon's hands on his shoulders, and he was both grateful and a little embarrassed to have her there.

Once he was able to compose himself enough to thread two sentences together, he prayed over his grandfather, thanking God for placing him in his life. "Bless his soul, God."

Even before he made to stand, a wad of tissues were placed in his hand, and he was warmed by Sharon's thoughtfulness. As horrible as the circumstances were, he was happy that his grandfather met her before he transitioned. None of his brothers had been able to make it fast enough; at least someone else witnessed those last minutes.

Bradley wiped and cleaned his face as much as the tissues would allow, then excused himself so he could finish in the restroom. Once he exited, he connected gazes with Sharon and held his hand out to her, needing the physical connection to keep him grounded one second, and off the floor weeping like a baby the next. Without a word, he led her out of the ICU.

Gregg and Kera stood by the waiting room door with expectant expressions, but he figured the look on his face said it all. Without a word, Gregg gave him a full hug, expressing his condolences for his loss.

"Gramps will surely be missed," whispered Gregg.

As much as Bradley tried to hold steady, his friend's words and hug crumbled his reserve, letting a few tears slip through his lashes.

***

Bradley was coming out of yet another bathroom when he noticed Dr. Williams standing with his friends. He gave Bradley a sad smile.

"Don't worry about anything; the nurse who tended to your grandfather will provide the information to the mortuary. I'll have them contact you as soon as they arrive. Again, I'm so sorry for your loss. Please take care of yourself and if you need anything, let us know."

Bradley nodded in thanks, struggling against a fresh round of tears at the thought of not being able to talk with Gramps anymore.

Dr. Williams turned and walked down the hall back to the ICU.

Bradley's relationship with his grandfather was special and unbreakable. Bradley was the only constant in Old Man DuPont's life since the death of Bradley's parents and grandmother. He dreaded the thought that his relationship with his grandfather would now only be memories, even though they would be mostly good ones.

Just as they were about to get on the elevator, Ken, the youngest of his two brothers, got off.

"Is Gramps okay?" he asked worriedly.

Bradley looked at his brother and shook his head, swallowing before replying, "No, brother. He passed away about a half hour ago."

Ken dropped to the floor, sobbing and crying. Bradley reached down, pulled him to his feet, and hugged him tightly, trying to give whatever comfort he could. Though his relationship with Gramps was filled with constant communication, no matter how many days passed between his brothers and grandfather talking, each of his brothers had their own special relationship with him and loved their grandfather dearly. It was he who stepped in to take care of them after the death of their parents. He taught them how to work hard and to be gentlemen. He kept them in church and taught them the essentials of life.

"Man, we don't have anybody else; what are we going to do?" Ken asked through his sobs.

Bradley looked up to the ceiling before looking back down at his brother and said, "We have each other. Come over to the house with me."

Ken shook his head to the negative and wiped his eyes on his shirt sleeve. "I'll come over tomorrow. I want to see Gramps one more time."

Bradley let him go. "Okay. You know I love you, and I'll always be here for you."

Ken nodded.

Bradley watched his brother slowly walk down the hall, his shoulders slumped as if he were carrying the weight of the world on them. He felt very much the same.

As he, Greg, Kera, and Sharon rode in the elevator to the lobby, which would take them to another elevator that led to the parking structure, he thought of the upcoming conversations he would have with his other brother, and he just felt tired. He resisted taking Sharon's hand again, not wanting to come off looking needy.

When the second set of elevator doors opened, he was at a momentary loss of where to go. With nothing left to do, the remaining group left the elevator and walked to their cars.

"I'll ride with you to keep you company," Gregg said, and Bradley didn't protest. He needed time to process what had just happened.

"Okay, that sounds good." He looked over at Sharon. "Can I talk to you for a moment?"

She turned to face him. "Sure."

Bradley observed every step she took as she walked towards him. His eyes traveled from her eyes to her pink-tipped toes in the pretty sandals and back up. It seemed inappropriate to notice how shapely her legs were in the pink sundress, but he did. Her hair flowed in the breeze that had entered the parking structure. She had this glow to her, emphasized by the dim parking lights. Still, her looks came in second to her heart, which he got a good glimpse of this evening. She was a special woman.

"Sharon, I really appreciate what you did for me in there. I know I put you in an awkward position, being that we just met today, and I apologize for that," he explained. He pulled her into a gentle embrace, rubbing his face against her hair, which was almost intoxicating to his senses before releasing her but keeping hold of one of her hands.

"It was kind of awkward at first, but after meeting your grandfather, he reminded me of Samuel, Kera's dad, who for all intents and purposes is my dad to."

"What do you mean? How is that? I mean. Where's your dad? Your parents? Are they still living?" he asked.

"No, my parents were killed in an accident years ago." she said.

"I'm so sorry, Sharon. How could I've been so insensitive? I shouldn't have asked you to go inside the room with me. Will you please forgive me?" The last thing in the world he wanted to do was to cause her any pain.

"It's okay; you didn't know."

He took a deep breath and put his hand over his chest. "I really am sorry. Now, I know this may sound crazy, but would you join me for lunch tomorrow?"

Sharon wanted to say, "Of course I will," but she didn't want to come off as desperate. She looked at Kera before looking back at him and said, "Well, I'm supposed to visit Kera's family for lunch tomorrow after church, and it's kind of a tradition."

Bradley looked disappointed, but he nodded. "I understand. Maybe some other time."

***

Kera and Gregg headed over to join them.

"Ladies, please treat yourself to some dinner," Gregg said, handing Kera his black card and kissing her softly. "I'm going to hang with the guys for a bit."

"Well, I'd better go," said Sharon, letting go of Bradley's hand. "I don't want to keep them waiting. If you want to talk, you can call me."

"I would love that," Bradley responded. They both smiled, and he pulled out his cell phone to put in her number.

After giving him the number, Sharon walked away.

As he opened his car door, Kera called out to Bradley, "Hey, my family is having dinner at my parents' house tomorrow after church, and we'd like it if you could come."

Bradley looked back at Sharon with a smile on his face. She was smiling, too. It seemed they were both happy that Kera invited him. He didn't want to seem too anxious by accepting quickly, even though this would give him and Sharon an opportunity to get closer. In his heart, he felt like the invitation was fate.

"Are you sure? I don't want to impose since this is a day that your family gets together."

"Nonsense!" exclaimed Kera. "You're family, and we would love to have you over. Besides, it would give someone an opportunity to eat Aunt Patsi's disgusting pound cake." Kera laughed.

"In that case, I would love to come. Thank you for inviting me," Bradley replied. Then they all laughed and said their goodbyes.

The corner of Sharon's lip lifted into a smile as she got into the car. Bradley DuPont was all she could think about on the drive back to Kera's parents' house.

Chapter Seven

THAT NIGHT, WHILE BRADLEY looked through the papers his grandfather told him about, thoughts of his childhood surfaced. He remembered all the times his father and grandfather would take him and his brothers fishing and canoeing during the summer. It was the most fun he and his brothers had together.

Reflections on conversations the old man had with them when he wanted to make them understand the importance of family, surfaced. His famous saying was, "There will be a time when Mom and Dad will close their eyes for the last time; then you'll only have each other. All hell can break loose in and around a family when the parents are gone, so make sure you tell each other that you care about them while you have the chance."

The hell did break loose, but the three brothers didn't follow all of Gramps' advice. He wished they were closer, especially him and Charles.

He couldn't think of any reason why his brother would have so much distaste for him. They came from the same genetic make-up, but they were as different as night and day.

Bradley walked into his grandfather's bedroom and found a set of clothing spread over the chair in the corner. The old man must have set them out for the next day before he had the heart attack. He placed his hand over his face and cried, He left the room without putting them away.

Bradley walked into the study and saw the letters his grandfather had mentioned at the hospital on the desk. He sat on the couch and read over them. Amongst the paperwork was an envelope. Turning it over, the contents spilled out to reveal his grandfather's last will and testament. It looked like his grandfather had the documents drawn up by his attorney five years ago.

As he read through it, he noticed that the old man had made sure to include each of the grandchildren, and he was very generous with them all, even though during their conversation, he had constantly said the only one deserving was Bradley. His grandfather had griped that he was more responsible with the family business and his own personal career.

Bradley sat for hours reading documents and trying to organize Gramps' affairs until he became exhausted by how much still needed to be done. He collapsed on a chair in the sitting area and turned on the television, only to have his mind drift to thoughts of Sharon. He had dated some beautiful women in his life—women from wealthy backgrounds and some who had made their own wealth. Women who knew how to have a good time and did all the things he enjoyed.

It wasn't all pleasant. In fact, one of them gave him his worst dating experience ever. In fact, she almost ruined his life, and he had to try so hard to forget her.

All of them lacked one important characteristic. Sadly, none of these women cared about him as a man, the man. They just cared about what they could get from him... Until now, he hadn't even thought of loving or caring for someone again.

Sharon wasn't like any of the women from his past relationships. She had shown him that she wasn't only beautiful on the outside but on the inside, as well. No other woman from his past would have dared to come into the room of a dying man they knew nothing about, not to mention coming to the hospital to show him they genuinely cared. To Bradley, that spoke volumes about who this woman was. He couldn't help wanting to get to know her more and seeing if she got better.

On Sunday morning, Bradley woke up to get ready for church. He knew that he needed to hear a good message today, and he knew he would get to spend some time with Sharon. He walked into the bathroom, turned on the shower, and then returned to the bedroom.

He wasn't sure what he wanted to wear. Most of his clothes were back at his home in Sacramento. He opened the closet and pulled out his black suit, with a purple shirt and a black tie that had purple, grey and white stripes on it. His Polo Ralph Lauren black loafers laid at the edge of the bed. He got out of his undergarments and laid them neatly on the bed. Then he walked into the bathroom to shower.

Once dressed, he grabbed some orange juice and headed out the door for church.

***

Gregg and Kera were already sitting when Bradley arrived at the church he sometimes attended with his grandfather. Gramps had been a member for years and whenever he came to visit, if he was still there on Sunday, he would come.

He walked over to where they were seated, and they made room for him in their row. He looked around and spotted Sharon on the third pew. *She looks so good.* Her long curls moved gracefully across her back as she turned her head from side to side. His thoughts were interrupted when he heard Pastor Carter ask the congregation to pray for the DuPont family during their time of bereavement. Bradley looked up to see his brother Charles sitting on the opposite side of the church. He wondered why Charles hadn't called to let him know he was coming into town, let alone return any of his calls regarding Gramps' heart attack. It shouldn't have taken him that long to drive from Raleigh to Columbia.

After service was over, Bradley watched for Charles even as he tried to keep an eye on Sharon. As he stared after him, Charles was trying to escape being seen by the pastor. Bradley was sure it had been several years since he'd been to church.

Bradley couldn't keep the smirk from his lips as the pastor side-stepped right in front of Charles, speaking to him briefly. The grin died, however, when the pastor turned around, looked straight at him, and ushered him over.

"I want to see you and Charles in my study for a few minutes after everyone leaves." Bradley nodded and looked over at his brother, who also nodded at the pastor but failed to look at him.

Bradley looked around for Sharon, hoping at least to say hi but couldn't find her in the crowd mingling outside the church. He would see her later. He would be patient.

He waited just inside but out of the way until the pastor was ready. "All right, boys. Come with me," his grandfather's pastor said as he walked past him with Charles in tow. His brother didn't say one word to Bradley, just looked at him and walked in with the pastor.

Once they were all seated, the pastor prayed. It was quick and gave mention of their relationship with their grandfather and him and his siblings, but Bradley was distracted by his brother's presence and had a hard time getting out of his head so he could pay more attention to the prayer.

"So, have you gentlemen decided on funeral arrangements for your grandfather?"

Bradley was momentarily at a loss for words. Wasn't that why they were here, so their grandfather's pastor could tell them how it would go? "I didn't have anything in particular in mind. I just want him taken care of in style. When I went through the documents he directed me to before he passed..." Bradley took a deep breath to calm his heart. Saying the words were like a sledgehammer to his gut. "When I looked through the papers on his desk last night, I found a contract with the mortuary. It looks like he thought of everything.

"Well, I don't care what the arrangements are as long as it happens fast," Charles cut in. "I have to get back to work soon."

Bradley was startled by his brother's stiff and unfeeling tone. He looked over at him, but Charles still refused to look at him.

He looked back at the pastor and shrugged. "I don't have a problem with that. We would just need help in letting everyone know when it is. Ken is already in town. He's staying at the house, so I'll see if he has anything he would like to add to the service."

The pastor continued to look between him and his brother and took a deep breath. He looked down at his desk at a huge calendar. "It's a weekday, but we have next Tuesday. That should be enough time to prepare the obituary and make arrangements with the mortuary and our bereavement ministries."

Bradley nodded, thankful that most of what the pastor mentioned was being taken care of due to his grandfather's planning.

"I encourage you to hold onto the legacy your grandfather and your family has built and not let the cares of this world keep you from experiencing the blessings of life."

Charles looked at the pastor and mumbled, "It's too late for that."

Bradley watched in disbelief, thinking how rude his brother was behaving, and again wondered why he was so hateful.

The pastor stared back at his brother for a moment before answering, "God's grace is sufficient, and His love is forever. You can't outrun it no matter how hard or fast you run."

Bradley shook his head and thought to himself, *I love my brother, but man, does he need a good swift kick in the butt.*

***

It was the men's turn to prepare dinner today, and Bradley smelled the food as he got out of his car, and boy, was he hungry. He couldn't wait to eat. Gregg had told him about Kera's parents' Sunday family gathering. He thought it was different that on this particular Sunday, the women would sit back while the men worked in the kitchen.

He also couldn't wait to see Sharon; the anticipation caused his palms to get clammy. He quickly walked to the door and when it opened, he was met with even heavier mouthwatering aromas.

"Hey, man," Gregg greeted him. "You disappeared after service. Kera and Sharon were looking for you."

The disappointment that came over Bradley was more intense than he would have liked. "I'm sorry I missed her. Pastor Carter wanted to meet with me and Charles, so I had to go to his study." He barely finished the sentence when he glanced over to see Sharon on the couch, talking with Kera.

Just as he imagined, she looked even more appealing in casual attire. He thought to himself that nothing so simple as jeans and a t-shirt could look more appealing on her. He was pretty sure he caught a glimpse of her walking through the crowd after church, but he hadn't been able to catch up to her. She wore a knee-length fitted black dress, accented with a red belt and accessories to match. Her heels made her legs look... Her laugh pulled him away from his thoughts. She whispered back and forth with her friend, and he was content to watch her until she stopped as if she was aware of being watched and turned, locking eyes with him. He couldn't think of any other place he'd rather be than right there in her presence.

"Okay. Well, if you're all good..." Gregg's sentence faded away as he continued to look at Sharon.

Bradley made his rounds with greetings and brief small talk, all the while keeping tabs on Sharon. It was only then that he gave himself permission to walk up to her.

"Hey, Sharon," he said, smiling down at her, noting the swinging of her crossed leg.

"Bradley," she greeted, mimicking his tone.

He grinned to himself. She seemed a little put off by his delay in coming to her. "How are you doing?"

"Good." Then her expression changed. It softened, and he wanted to shield himself so he wouldn't embarrass himself because of what he saw in her eyes. "How are you doing?"

He shrugged, no longer trusting himself to talk.

He watched as she uncrossed her legs, got up from the couch, and offered him her hand, saying, "Come on."

He glanced down at her hand and took a deep breath before enveloping her hand in his. He let her lead him back out of the front door. She sat on a bench on the front porch and motioned for him to sit next to her. She turned to him, and the intensity of her gaze made him feel exposed.

"I know I hardly know you, but I'm willing to listen if you need someone to talk to."

He looked at her for a moment, trying to measure how sincere she was and if taking her up on her offer would bring them closer or send her running. *Wouldn't now be a better time to find out if she had staying power?* He took a deep breath and took Sharon up on her offer.

He shared a little about his family and the important role his grandfather played in his life, then he told her about what happened that morning after church. When he was done, Sharon stared at him for a few seconds before moving in closer to him and wrapping him in a hug. For the first time in a long time, he took the warmth and comfort a woman gave without wondering what they wanted in return. *She wasn't a runner.*

When it was time to eat, he made sure to grab a seat next to Sharon. He could barely pay attention to the spread because of the woman beside him.

Bradley would look up from his plate from time to time to catch Sharon's eye. Once he looked up to see everyone watching him and Sharon and noticed that it didn't faze him. His first thought wasn't trying to backpedal or deny what was happening. I just wanted to settle into it and see what could happen.

After an afternoon of good food, laughter, and talking, the end of the day was fast approaching.

When it was time to leave, Sharon figured she would get a head start by putting together a portfolio for the meeting so that nothing would be missed. Her thoughts caused a sense of anxiety to come over her as she remembered that she didn't drive to church. Kera had picked her up, and she didn't want her friend to have to leave her family just to take her home. She and Kera had a very important meeting at work the next morning. It could be their biggest client yet. A wealthy businesswoman was coming to discuss them decorating the new home she'd built on the lake. Both ladies were equally excited about the referral from one of their most prominent clients. Their business would be even more successful with this client.

"I'll call an Uber to take me home. I don't want to pull you from your family."

"It's all good. I don't have a problem leaving, especially since Aunt Patsi wants to share her stories about her rendezvous in Europe."

Sharon knew most of the family were entertained by Aunt Patsi, which included herself on occasion. She was a woman who enjoyed life to its fullness, without a care about the consequences.

Bradley stepped into their small circle. "If you need a ride home, Sharon, I can give you one. Sharon had enjoyed her time with Bradley, but even with him showing his vulnerable side, her insecurities kicked in, which made her suspicious of his motives. *Does he want to get me alone?* He seemed nice enough, but that could have been because people were around. Maybe he was a crazy person, showing them one side of himself, but deep down, he was a deranged lunatic.

She shrugged off her thoughts and responded, "I don't want to put you out. Really, I can call a service to pick me up."

"It's not a problem." He turned to Kera. " In fact, it would be my pleasure to make sure she makes it home safely."

Kera looked at Sharon with a smile and gave her a wink. Sharon immediately knew what her friend was thinking. She tilted her head to the side with a look, as if to say *I'm not falling for this*. Her memories of Mark resurfaced, but after a slight hesitation, she agreed to let him take her home.

Chapter Eight

WHILE DRIVING HOME FROM dinner, Bradley turned the station to the Quiet Storm on the Big DM 101.3 FM. Slow jams from the 90s were playing. Sharon obviously recognized the current song and nodded her head to the beat, humming the lyrics in her head. Bradley glanced over at her and sighed. He had to keep from staring as she gave herself over to the lyrics and rhythm. As she looked away, he noticed her lips had parted into a wide grin.

As Bradley turned onto the paved driveway leading up to Sharon's house, Sharon shifted her hips nervously in the passenger seat. Her mind rehearsed what she would say to him while trying to quickly exit Bradley's late-model Wagoneer truck.

Once he pulled up in front of her house, Bradley switched off the car engine, got out of the car, and walked swiftly around to the passenger side to open the door for her. His feet appeared to be in skipping mode, full of happiness. She could see him in the side mirror, approaching her door as she tried to compose herself. Then the door opened, as Bradley stood in front of her.

Sharon knew that no matter what her plans were for getting out of being so close to Bradley, it was too late. She placed her right leg out of the car and proceeded to turn her body to get up from the seat, when she realized she was being held back. The strap on her purse had somehow gotten caught on the gear shift as she tried to exit the vehicle. He reached into the car to help release her.

Sharon's breathing grew faster. She couldn't help but be taken in by the intoxicating cologne he wore. She tried hard to keep some distance between them as he leaned out of the car and held out his hand to assist her from the car.

Bradley escorted her up the front steps, taking in the most beautiful garden lights lining the walkway all the way to the door, where smaller lights illuminated the doorway. They stood in front of the welcome sign on her front porch. Adjacent to the door on the right was a potted flowerpot she had decorated, filled with red, yellow, and purple geraniums.

Bradley positioned himself in a military stance. She could tell he hoped the night wouldn't end with just a simple goodbye.

Sharon turned away from him so she could retrieve her house keys from her purse. She turned her head slightly to look at him, observing the way he stood as if he were her personal bodyguard. Boy was he a bodyguard she would love to have protecting her. Knowing he was there made her feel secure.

"I think I'll go in now. Thank you for bringing me home," she said. The angular curve of his jaw loosened, and a salacious grin formed on his mouth.

"What is it?" asked Sharon. She could tell by the way he looked at her that he had something he wanted to say.

He took a step closer to her and whispered in a deep husky tone, "You're one of the most beautiful and sexy woman I've ever met."

Yeah, right. How many other women have you said this too?

Before she could continue with the conversation in her head, he pulled her close to him, running his thumbs up and down her arms.

"I've been waiting to kiss you ever since the first time I saw you." He ran his fingers down the side of her face. "May I kiss you?"

She was at a loss for words. She wanted this kiss but was afraid she would end up in the same situation she worked so hard to get out of. He slipped his hand to the back of her head, cradling the nape of her neck in his palm. She watched him, spellbound for one, two, three heartbeats, feeling much like a deer caught in headlights. She gave a small nod. Then he took ownership of her mouth with his, making every nerve in her body paralyzed.

His hand glided along her spine with a soft touch, yet firm enough to make her limp in his arms. The message her body sent to her brain overrode every sense of reality that made her unable to fight against those emotions. This one man made her feel she had little to no control over herself when he was around. She couldn't change it even if she wanted.

Bradley could tell she enjoyed his kisses and wanted to make sure she understood how much he enjoyed kissing her. The look on Sharon's face told him everything he needed to know, and this made him satisfied. He slowly removed his lips from hers but still held her close. The look she gave him tugged at his heartstrings, and he wondered if they were destined to be together.

Suddenly, Bradley's phone vibrated. He removed it from his pocket and looked at the number; it was his brother Ken. Still feeling the warmth of each other, he said in a low and sultry tone, "I need to answer this call, babe."

To a degree, she was happy for the distraction. Sharon nodded in agreement and slowly pulled from his embrace. Had they stayed wrapped in each other's arms, only God knew what would have happened.

"I'm coming, man. Just stay put. I'm on the way!"

"Is everything okay?"

"Yes. My brother is at the house, but he forgot his key. Regrettably, I have to leave." His expression faded from cheerful to concerned.

Regrettably? She thought. Sharon hated hearing him say he had to leave, but the warmth in his voice gave her some peace.

"Okay." She nodded. "Thank you again for the ride home."

Bradley didn't want to leave her without making her understand how much he wanted nothing more than to spend more time with her. He leaned in and kissed her softly on the lips.

"I really enjoyed myself and just as I expected, you taste as good as you look. I hope the next time we meet, it will be just as enjoyable," he whispered.

"I hope so too." Sharon gazed into his eyes.

She watched from her front door window, as he drove down her driveway and out of sight.

I hope so too, she pondered *Oh boy, I'm in for it now. I can't allow myself to be tempted into another man's world only to get hurt again.*

No matter how hard she tried to convince herself that it wouldn't work between her and Bradley, she could only think about the way he held her when they kissed. She remembered the last conversation she and Kera had about her finding her Boaz also. *Could Bradley DuPont be my Boaz?* She mused. She hadn't surrendered her ability to trust her heart to another human being, especially after the last man she was in a relationship with. Sharon knew she'd have to learn how to love again one day. She also knew that her flesh was weak and growing weaker every time she was in close contact with Bradley.

Bradley drove on the interstate, heading to his grandfather's house. His thoughts reflected on Sharon and the way she made him feel inside. He felt a sense of peace when he was near her. To hear her voice made him feel like he could pour out his innermost thoughts, knowing they were safe with her. He had never felt this way before about any woman, he thought that she could be the one he could let down his guard with. He couldn't get her out of his mind the entire drive home, and listening to the slow music in the background as he cruised along didn't help, either.

When Bradley reached his grandfather's home, he found his brother lying asleep on the front porch. Ken was the drifter in the family. He would show up in the blink of an eye, and then he would be gone just as quickly, for weeks on end.

As he approached the bench where Ken lay, he thought about a time when Ken was about five years old. *Ah, sweet memories those were.* Those moments were full of love and warmth. When Ken was frightened by their darkened bedroom, he would jump in bed with Bradley just so he would feel safe. It seemed like things never changed.

"Ken," he whispered, trying not to scare him awake. "I'm here. Come let's go inside." His brother sat up looking groggy and unfocused. It was a few seconds before he saw his brother's eyes cleared, and Bradley could tell he recognized where he was.

"Come on," he repeated and helped his brother up and into the house. He led him to the den where he let Ken sprawl out on the couch while he took the loveseat.

They sat for hours reminiscing and talking about the good times they shared as young boys. They laughed and even cried together as the night gave way to the next morning.

After a couple of hours of sleep, Bradley rose to make sure he had time to prepare breakfast for his brother before heading out to a meeting. Ken promised him that he would be there when he returned. For once, Bradley knew he was telling the truth. Ken shared the night before that he had been evicted from his last residence.

Chapter Nine

Sharon tossed and turned throughout the night. Her mind was consumed with the events that transpired throughout the day between her and Bradley. She didn't want to admit that she was falling for him, but she knew she had to control herself when they were in each other's presence. That would be difficult; they would see each other more, as their two best friends were getting married, and they now had a physical connection. The physical tension in her body made her realize that she missed having the caressing touch of a man.

She still felt his lips pressed against hers from last night's kiss. Suddenly, images of her own wedding day bloomed as she became Mrs. Bradley DuPont one day. The honeymoon would be the most exciting part of it all. She could give herself completely to him, without any feelings of guilt and shame.

Sharon chuckled at the thought, swiftly erasing it from her mind. She couldn't allow herself to be pulled in by another man. She had trailed this path before, and it got her nowhere fast. She had allowed herself to be used and got caught up in a relationship she knew wasn't healthy for her.

Sharon was an old-fashioned girl with traditional values, even though her life had somehow steered in a different direction from how she was raised. She remembered the kind of relationship her parents had. When her father looked at her mother, it was with pure adoration. He would surprise her with vacations for no reason at all and when she would walk into her office, it'd be full of flowers. Her mother had shown her one of the cards that accompanied her father's gesture on one such occasion. It read, "I love you just because you're you."

Her father was spontaneous and caring that way. Sharon felt she deserved the same kind of romance in her life that her father gave to her mother.

Mark had started out that way, but towards the end, he only showed that type of affection when he felt her slipping away from him, and only because of a guilty conscience. He didn't do it because he loved her; he just wanted to keep her strung along. He was convinced that he had her in his hip pocket, and she would always be there, putting up with his mess. The next morning, Sharon felt the sting of having woken up so early after such a restless night. She was exhausted but enthusiastic about the events that were about to take place in her life. With thoughts of Bradley and the firm's new client, Catherine Morris, her excitement reached an all-time high.

With the excitement came anxiety. She wanted to make the best possible impression on Catherine.

As Sharon stepped out of the shower, she heard her phone ringing. She quickly wrapped a towel around herself before reaching for it.

"Are you on your way?"

"No. I overslept. I should be there in a half hour with the plans and projections," Sharon replied as she picked out a black and teal wraparound dress and black heels to wear to the meeting.

"Okay, cool. I'm already here. I couldn't sleep. I was so excited, I wanted to make sure everything was perfect. I won't delay you any longer."

"All right, girl. Calm down. Maybe drink some decaf. I'll be there soon," Sharon said, rubbing herself down with her towel.

"Okay. Yeah, maybe I should switch to decaf. I'll see you soon."

As she applied her makeup, she wondered how Bradley was doing and whether she should give him a quick call.

She picked up her cell phone to call him, but as she made the call, she noticed him calling her.

She smiled and immediately answered the call, "Hello, Sharon speaking."

"Good morning, sunshine. I just wanted to call you this morning to see if you had a good night's rest last night."

Sharon swallowed a bit before answering; a flashback of the kiss they shared the night before came across her mind.

"I slept okay she lied. Thank you for asking," "How are you today, Bradley?"

"I'm about as well as expected. My brother and I went through some of our grandfather's things, talked a while, and sorted out some things. It was rough, but we managed. Thanks."

She wondered if he felt the way she did. *Did he want to tell her how much he enjoyed her company as she had his?*

"I really enjoyed our time together yesterday."

Sharon was surprised to hear the same word she was thinking come out of his mouth. ""Me too," she said, taking the plunge.

"I was wondering..." Sharon's phone beeped with the notification of an incoming call.

"I'm sorry for interrupting. Would you please hold on for me? It's Kera."

"Sure, baby."

"Hey, Kera. What's up?"

"Hey, our client's flight was delayed due to bad weather."

Sharon paused in applying her makeup, her heart plummeting. They were so close.

"She still wants to meet with us though, so she asked if we could push back the meeting to three o'clock because the client's flight was delayed due to weather. I told her that was fine, but that I needed to check your schedule to make sure you didn't have any meetings scheduled that I didn't know about."

Sharon breathed a sigh of relief. "Three is fine. I don't have anything besides paperwork today."

"Good. I'll let her know. See you later," Kera said with a happy cheer.

"Thanks, Kera!" Sharon responded with gratitude, then she took a deep breath and returned to her call with Bradley.

"Is everything all right?" he asked.

"Yes, it was Kera letting me know our appointment was rescheduled to later this afternoon," she stated.

"Well, since your meeting is postponed, would you accompany me to lunch? My treat."

"That sounds nice," she said, trying to sound as nonchalant as possible though she was absolutely giddy.

"I'll pick you up at eleven forty-five so that we can be at the restaurant by twelve-thirty. Does that work for you?"

"Yes. That works. Where are you taking me?"

"To lunch at a restaurant. The rest you'll find out when we arrive."

"Really?"

"Really. This will take a little trust," Bradley said quietly.

Sharon didn't know how to respond at first. She swallowed back the reservation. "Okay."

"Good. I'll see you in a few hours."

"See you in a few hours. I'll be ready," Sharon replied.

When she hung up the phone with Bradley, she ran into her closet and pulled out a red sleeveless dress with peek-a-boo slits at her shoulders, between her collarbone and cleavage and between her lowest rib and waist on both sides. She didn't want to seem desperate, so she put it back on the hanger. It had been six months since she'd gone out on a date and much longer since a first date. She looked over to the side of her closet that had casualwear and decided to play it safe by wearing a simple black romper with V-shaped back and low strapped sandals that complemented the shape of her legs. *Perfect.*

The last thing Sharon wanted was to make him feel like she was trying hard to be noticed, but it was too late. The kiss they shared gave every indication that she was very interested in him.

Sharon looked at the clock and forced herself to concentrate on the present and her time with Bradley. She had plenty of time after their lunch to get nervous about their potential client. Didn't she already have enough to be nervous about? There was a war going on within her. The battle between what she wanted and what she needed. She wanted more long looks, more conversation, and more kisses from Bradley, but she needed to take things slow and get to know him better. She needed to trust her judgement. Sharon gave herself one last look in the mirror and felt good about what she saw. She would work on the inside later.

Bradley arrived at Sharon's on time. When she opened the door, he was at a loss for words. The sight of her almost made him stop breathing. He wondered how the Creator of the world had designed such a woman, with brains *and* beauty. His heart leaped every time he was in her presence. She had all the qualities a man could want. He knew she was special, and it would take a special kind of man to appreciate such a rarity.

"You look amazing!" He stared into her eyes as he complimented her. He chided himself because he felt the tone in his voice didn't hide his admiration or want at all.

She looked down, her cheeks turning red at his compliment. He found it endearing. How could she not know how beautiful she was?

"Thank you, Bradley. You look as handsome as ever."

He walked her to the car and just before she was about to get in, he leaned in and gently kissed her. "Just wanted to say good morning properly," he whispered, watching as her eyes danced with happiness.

"Do you like Japanese food?" Bradley asked, while positioning himself in the driver's seat.

"Yes," she replied. The monosyllabic response caused Bradley to look over to see if she was having reservations but upon seeing her snuggle deeper into the passenger seat of his car, he felt a sense of pride that she would relax and trust that he would get them to their destination without incident.

He allowed her to relax a little while he pulled onto the street and maneuvered his way into the light late-morning traffic. Once he was on the straightaway, he glanced over at Sharon who seemed to be in her head. He was no long content.

"Penny for your thoughts." He watched her turn away from the window she'd been looking out of.

"I'm just trying to stay in the moment and enjoy this time..." She closed her mouth though he was sure she had more to say. He wondered if he was imagining that she would say, "with you." It only instilled a determination to keep her in the moment.

"I'm glad you agreed to come out with me this morning. It's been a tense time for me, as you know, so this is a bright spot in my day. You're a bright spot," he finished, making sure to meet her eyes before returning his gaze to the road.

He watched the smile take over her features

Wanting to keep things light, even though he wanted to know all there was to know about Sharon, he began with easy questions. "So, now that I know you like Japanese food, what's your favorite food period?" He glanced over to see Sharon bite her lip in concentration.

"Mmm. Kera's mom Sara makes the best five cheese macaroni and cheese. I could eat it for breakfast, lunch, and dinner, but then I wouldn't be able to get out of my door. What about you? What's your favorite food?"

Bradley thought about the question for only a couple of seconds before the memory of his grandfather's gumbo ran through his mind. "My grandfather made the best gumbo. He made the rue from scratch, then added some Louisiana-style hotlinks, Dungeness crab, chicken wings, jumbo shrimp, and sweet corn." He could practically smell it, and it made his stomach rumble.

"That sounds so good. You have my mouth watering. Did you ever make it with him?"

"A couple of times." He checked his mirrors before changing lanes. "He was one of those all-day cookers. He could spend hours preparing that dish. Had the whole house filled with the aroma hours before it was ready. It would drive me and my brothers crazy." He chuckled to himself. "One time Ken snuck into the pot before it was ready and got a burnt tongue and a toasted backside after Grams found out."

Sharon giggled, shaking her head. "I know what you mean. My mom used to make gingerbread cookies. They smelled so good, but it only took once for me to try to sneak a bite before they were done cooling."

"Did you get punished?"

"No. I think my mom thought my burnt tongue was punishment enough." She shrugged. "I'm glad you have good memories of your grandfather. He seemed like a really good man."

"He was our safe place to land," he said, feeling a lump grow in his throat. He needed a distraction. "What else did your mother make?"

Sharon caught his eyes for a moment, seeming to understand his struggle. She smiled at him and told him about some of her mother's recipes and her antics as a little girl. Before long, he pulled into the parking lot of the restaurant, more than grateful for her compassion.

Reaching his hand out to hers after opening her door, Bradley breathed in her vanilla scent and was instantly mesmerized.

Sharon daydreamed of his arms wrapping around her waist and pulling her close. She almost blushed when the waiter interrupted her imagination to seat them at a table.

"What can I start you off with this afternoon?" the waiter asked.

"We'll have two glasses of your best wine and some water, please," said Bradley.

Sharon looked at him, "Don't you think it's a little early to have wine?"

"No, I thought it would make it easier for both of us to relax," he responded.

"I'm all for relaxing. The meeting for this afternoon has me feeling on edge."

"I know you're going to give a great presentation, and you'll get the contract. I have faith in you. Anyone would be crazy not to have you be their interior designer." Bradley's face lit up with enthusiasm.

"Thank you; that means a lot to me." Sharon smiled, and he watched as she looked around the restaurant, taking in the art on the walls and the small Japanese garden outside the restaurant's back wall of windows. He was content to watch her take it all in until their waiter came back with their wine.

He said nothing as she took a sip of her wine—a full-bodied cabernet he knew to be the perfect balance of bitter and sweet.

The wine was perfect, the atmosphere was relaxing, and the sushi was delicious. It was a perfect setting for an early-afternoon date. Sharon and Bradley laughed and talked through their entire lunch, enjoying each other's company.

All too soon, the bottle was empty, and the last piece of nigiri was eaten. Bradley put his napkin on top of his plate and shifted forward in his chair. "We'd better get going so you won't be late for your meeting. I hope you enjoyed your lunch, and if you want, can we do this again soon?"

"I had a wonderful time, Bradley. You're quite the gentlemen." As if she expected anything less from him. "I would very much like to do this again."

Sharon wasn't sure whether she was dreaming. She could hardly breathe at the thought that, just maybe, this was her chance at love and happiness.

Once they arrived at her home, Bradley walked Sharon to her front door. Sharon placed her key in the door and slowly turned towards him. She thanked him again for a lovely afternoon. Before she could say more, he took her into his arms and kissed her ever so gently. She could barely think. All she could do was respond to him in hopes he would sense the depth of her feelings for him. She felt helpless when she was around him.

He pulled her tighter to him. She felt the warmth of his lips as they massaged hers with every kiss he gave. He backed her up against the door and when it didn't give, she realized she had never opened it, let alone unlocked it. Sharon summoned all of her strength to pull out of the fog Bradley surrounded her in. "I nee... I need to open the door. I would rather not give my neighbors a show." She felt his arms loosen, and she turned to unlock the door.

She was barely two steps into the foyer when she felt him step up behind her. She heard the door close, and she was turned back in his arms being caressed from the nape of her neck to her lower back .

When he slid his hands up the side of her body, Sharon felt a hot flash come over her as if she were in a sauna turned up over one hundred and seventy-five degrees.

She held him tightly as their breathing grew faster and faster. She felt there was no way out of this situation, for they both wanted the same thing. He lowered his mouth from hers, heading down to her neck while his hands massaged her hips.

I must do something. I can't allow myself to get into the same situation again.

Her thoughts were interrupted by his hand sliding up the front of her thigh.

She remembered what a wise older woman said to her when she was a young lady, "Child, once you taste the gravy, it's hard to go back to plain rice." She was right. She did want the gravy on the rice but not like this. Not without having a commitment from someone who loved her unconditionally.

Oh, how weak the flesh is.

Boy, was hers getting weaker by the minute.

In a low, deep tone, he said to her, "I want you, Sharon. You're all I think about. Would you please let me love you? I promise to make you feel like the woman you deserve to be."

With a sigh, she said to him, "I want you too, Bradley."

At her words, he gently lifted her off the floor and into his arms. He carried her into the living room and placed her on the couch. He ran one hand up the front of her rib cage and cupped the underside of her breast.

Just then, her phone rang. Both she and Bradley tried to ignore the ringing in her purse and couldn't find the strength to break contact. Bradley pulled the straps of her romper down, to expose the top part of her chest. He kissed her neck until it felt like time stood still for hours, surrounding them with a peaceful atmosphere.

She couldn't stop her hands from stroking his biceps, as she was caught up in the lust-filled spell he had woven around them. With every ring of her phone, her heart beat faster and faster. She wanted him just as badly as he wanted her. She opened her eyes to glance at him, watching how involved he was in pleasing her. She looked at the clock on the wall to find a way to break the powerful hold he seemed to have on her. It was approaching one thirty, and she knew she had to get ready for her meeting.

The phone rang again, and the ringtone told her it was Kera calling her back. She knew she had to break free from Bradley's passionate touches; otherwise, there was no turning back.

"I can't..." she murmured.

He continued kissing her, not hearing a word she said. "I can't," she repeated.

He gazed up at her and said, "You can't? Are you sure? I'll stop if you want, but I really don't think you want me to."

Trying to think straight enough to say the words, she stuttered, "We... we have to... to stop. I have to get ready for my meeting."

Bradley pressed himself harder to her and kissed her with such passion, she felt as if every nerve in her body was paralyzed. Slowly, he released his lips from hers. Holding her in his arms, he breathed the words, "I find it so hard to leave you. You make me forget all the pain I ever had. I want to tell you something..."

The ringing of her cell phone interrupted him.

"I have to answer the phone, baby."

Bradley agreed but with a disappointed look on his face. He got up so she could search for her purse.

She moved around the living room in a drunken haze of passion, trying to make her body listen to her sluggish brain. When she was far enough from Bradley, coherent thought kicked in, and she followed the sound of her ringtone to her purse lying on the floor in the doorway. "Kera, what's wrong?" Sharon asked once she picked up her phone.

"You're on your way here? I thought we were going to meet at the office."

"Yes, but I would like to compare notes and get a strategy in place for how we can get this contract. I should be over in ten minutes," Kera replied.

"Okay," Sharon answered. As she ended the call, she saw Bradley getting ready to leave and apologized for the interruption. She noticed that he was distracted and asked what he wanted to tell her.

"It can wait, beautiful. Get ready for your meeting, and I'll call you later." He bent down and kissed her much softer and slower than before. He leisurely traversed her mouth, eliciting new feelings in her.

She liked this tender side. It was even more alluring than the hot and urgent passion they shared just a mere minutes before.

When he finally released her, she looked up into his dark eyes, wishing she didn't have the meeting. "I should be finished with my day by six, and maybe we can meet for dinner," said Sharon, giving him a shrug, suddenly feeling shy.

"Tonight, I have to meet with my brothers to discuss the plans for the funeral." His voice, which had been deep and intense, now sounded distracted and full of a different type of emotion.

She placed a hand on his chest to relay her sympathy. "I understand. Let me know if there's anything I can do for you, Bradley."

"I appreciate that, baby. If I can get away for a few, I'll try to stop by and see you, if that's okay. I can't make any promises though, since it took everything inside me to get my brothers to agree for all of us to be in the same house, let alone in the same room, without wanting to fight." He smiled more to himself.

"Goodbye for now," he said before giving her one quick peck, then turning to walk to his car.

"Goodbye for now," she echoed. Swallowing hard to keep from protesting, Sharon watched as Bradley got into his car and headed out the driveway. The intense heat he left behind from his touches could still be felt in her.

Chapter Ten

Sharon rushed to get dressed, knowing Kera would show up and speculate about what she believed was going on between her and Bradley. Although the two were thick as thieves, Sharon didn't want her friend to get her hopes up too high if things didn't work out with Bradley. She needed to keep things simple and moving slowly.

Inside, she knew it was too late. Thoughts of how she allowed herself yet again to be put in the same position flowed through her mind.

As she prepared to put on her makeup, Kera came into the bedroom and stopped in the doorway of the bathroom, smiling as if she'd just received money she wasn't expecting. Sharon looked at her shyly, feeling the guilt of having spent a romantic afternoon with the man she found way too appealing.

"How are things going this afternoon?" Kera asked.

"Things are good, just trying to get ready for this meeting."

"Uh-huh," she responded. Kera turned to peruse the room for any sign of something unusual.

"What's wrong with you?" asked Sharon.

"Nothing, really. It's just that I saw Mr. DuPont leaving your driveway when I pulled up." She rubbed her hands together as she sat on the edge of the bed, situating herself as if she were preparing herself for all the juicy gossip.

Sharon gave her a look of confusion as if she knew nothing about what Kera was hinting at. She'd hoped that Kera wouldn't notice Bradley leaving her house, as she knew she would have some explaining to do. Her friend would want to know every detail leading up to that moment, and she'd have to tell her, or she would never hear the end of it.

"Yes, you're correct. It was Bradley leaving," Sharon admitted.

"I knew there was something going on between you two. I told Gregg that you guys were acting suspicious yesterday, *and* we would have to keep an eye on both of you." She laughed as she spoke.

Sharon didn't give her friend time to gloat; she admitted that she and Bradley had spent some time together for lunch, and they'd had a great time .

"Do tell," Kera said. "I want to know every intricate detail. Leave nothing out." She plopped down on the bed, all ears to hear the juiciest gossip ever.

"Well, when you called this morning and told me that the meeting with the client was pushed back, Bradley phoned as well and asked if he could take me out to lunch. We went to that Japanese restaurant downtown. For the first time in a long time, I felt like a man listened and understood me. We connect in so many ways. This is something I can't say even for Mark. He makes me feel safe and cared for." Sharon looked at Kera confidently, feeling a great sense of peace.

"Oh my," cried Kera. "You're in love with Bradley! This is great news! I'm so happy I'm speechless." She jumped up and hugged her friend, then danced around the room with vivacity.

"I wouldn't go that far, but that man has a way about him that makes me feel like I can do anything whenever I'm in his presence. Not to mention when he kisses me, girl—"

Kera abruptly stopped jumping around and interrupted her, "Hold up, what do you mean when he kisses you? Someone's been holding out on me. Do you mean to tell me that this isn't the first time? I thought we were like sisters, and you didn't tell me?" Kera held her head down and threw her hands in the air in disbelief. "I knew there was more going on between you two than just having casual conversations."

"It wasn't like that, Kera," Sharon said apologetically, wondering how much she had hurt her friend and what she could say to convince her friend that she hadn't been hiding anything.

Kera looked at her and burst into loud laughter. "Girl, I'm not tripping. Remember I know you better than anyone in this world. I knew there was something going on; every time he came around, your eyes lit up, and your chest would rise and fall as if you were out of breath. I'm just so happy for you, and you know I only want nothing but the best for you. You're my sister."

Sharon looked over at the clock on the dresser. "Oh, look at the time. We'll have to postpone our talk until after we go over the information you brought for the meeting with Ms. Morris."

"Don't think for one minute you're getting off that easy. You're going to fill me in on your hot steamy romance," said Kera. "No cheap detours around the details either. I want every bit of the juicy scenes." They both laughed.

Sharon got dressed while Kera went over key points she wanted to make sure they agreed on in presenting Ms. Morris. By the time they walked out the door, Sharon was confidently dressed to impress and looking forward to giving their client a proposal she would have a hard time refusing.

About an hour later, they arrived at the office. Kera turned to Sharon and said, "I still want full details of what happened between you two. I haven't forgotten."

"Don't I know it." Sharon gave her a slight smile.

When the office phone's intercom chimed, and Kera's receptionist announced the guest, they both looked at each other, took deep breaths, grabbed their notebooks, and walked into the lobby.

"Good afternoon, Ms. Morris. It's a pleasure to finally meet you in person. I'm Sharon Gable, and this is my partner, Kera Prescott."

"Good afternoon, ladies. Call me Catherine." She held her hand out with the fingers down like she was royalty. "I can see we're all going to be good friends. You have a lovely office, and I like the exquisite details of your designs. I know I'm in great hands."

Catherine exuded beauty and allure, yet Kera could sense a hidden resolve. Her eyes were sharp and a little too intense for Kera's comfort, but she didn't know this woman from Eve, so she told herself to relax.

"Okay, Catherine it is," responded Sharon. They shook hands, and Kera led the way to the boardroom where they were set up for the presentation.

As they walked through the boardroom door, Kera spoke to Catherine, "We'd like to know if you have any children and/or if you're planning on having a family. We ask this question, just so we'd have an idea of what we may need to consider when planning the final designs."

Catherine turned to look at them with a bewildered expression.

"Yes, we have a three-year-old son. His father travels a lot for work and isn't around much. We decided it would be best for us to move here so we could be close enough for him to build a bond with our son. This house is for us and our future together. He's the reason I made the transition here. They both mean the world to me."

"Oh, you're married? We didn't know that." Kera looked over at Sharon with curiosity. They were both amazed, seeing as she never said anything before.

"I'm not married yet; this is the reason for me moving here so we can be close to my fiancé. We wanted to give our child the experience of having a loving two-parent home."

"That's wonderful, Catherine!" said Sharon. "There's nothing like having a family. I believe it makes the world so much better to live in. I pray that things will work out for you, and we hope to meet your little boy soon. He could help us with the decorations for his room." Sharon smiled at her.

"Thank you. I'm sure he would love that very much," replied Catherine.

Two hours later, they finished their presentation. The meeting was a success. Catherine seemed to be in love with the plans they had put together for her new home.

"I want to thank you for all that you've done," said Catherine. "I can't wait to see the finished product. I wasn't sure you would be willing to pick up where the last designer left off, but you've improved upon my original concept. I've never seen anything so beautiful. Chicago has some wonderful designers, but I've never come across anything so phenomenal. It really does take my breath away. Now that we've finalized colors, textures and upholstery materials."

"We're so pleased to hear that," said Kera. "We like to think of our clients as family. We meticulously and thoughtfully put together what we felt our clients would be pleased with. After all, your home is your sanctuary. We know that once you see the end results, you'll be more than pleased with what we have in store for your home."

"Well, we're excited for you," said Kera. "You'll find that the Metro is a great place to live. It's growing and expanding, and we're close to everything... Charleston, Charlotte, Atlanta. Let us know if you need anything, and we'll be happy to show you around."

"Thank you so much," said Catherine. "That means a lot, Catherine." They shook hands, and Kera and Sharon walked her to the elevator.

Kera stood in front of the elevator for a few more seconds, wondering if the feelings that there was something slightly off with the woman could be credited to any one thing. She shook her head as she walked back towards her office.

"What's going on in that head of yours?" Sharon asked.

"I can't quite wrap my mind around it yet, but something isn't clicking with me about Catherine, and I'm not getting a good vibe from her."

"What do you mean?"

Kera saw Sharon watching her but couldn't place the source of the feeling in her gut. As she continued to replay the meeting in her mind, one instance waved a red flag at her conscience. "I just can't help but feel there's something off, especially her story about her fiancé. Did you see how her face changed when she spoke of him? It was really creepy."

"I'm not sure what you mean, but if you say so. I didn't see anything curious about what she said. She just seems like a woman who wants to rectify her life. Besides, if she makes good on our deal, I don't care who she is."

Kera looked at her friend. "All this talk about work has made me hungry. Can we please order some food?"

Even though Sharon was still somewhat full from lunch, she wanted to celebrate with her partner. She could always find something to snack on. "Sure. I'll get some of the menus, and we can choose something."

"Perfect," said Kera.

Chapter Eleven

Bradley prepared for his brothers' arrival. He hope that this time they would all act like civilized men and come together to get their grandfather buried. He wanted to have the funeral in two days; that way, the brothers wouldn't be in each other's presence longer than necessary. Even though he noticed the distance between him and his brothers steadily growing over the years , his love never changed, and he wanted to find out what was going on between them.

The doorbell rang, and he turned to look through the tempered glass framed in the door. The image was distorted but tall and broad enough to be recognized as Charles. He walked slowly to the door, took a deep breath, and opened it.

"Hello, Charles. I'm glad you made it."

"Bradley," Charles responded, sounding disgruntled. He walked briskly into the sitting room, where the family had many meetings when they were younger.

Bradley followed him into the room. Memories came to him of the times their grandfather would sit around the fire and tell them how to be the best men they could be. He could hear the voice of the old man echoing throughout the house as he looked at the pictures on the wall of him and his brothers in happier moments.

He looked over to see his older brother watching him with sadness and anger all over him.

"Where is Ken? I would have thought the kid would be here before me," Charles asked.

"He'll be here; I spoke with him over an hour ago. In the meantime, I prepared your old bedroom for you. When he gets here, we all can go fishing and catch some dinner. I went out and got everything we need," replied Bradley.

Just as Charles was about to say something, Ken came into the room.

"What's going on, my brothers?" he asked, in a loud and boisterous tone.

It was apparent that he had been drinking, and he looked like he hadn't bathed in a few days. His T-shirt was dingy and wrinkled, his sneakers looked as if he had been wallowing in a pig pen, and he reeked of alcohol. Stumbling into the sitting room, he tripped over the runner and fell onto the sofa.

"Ken, what in the world is wrong with you?" Charles asked. "You need to get yourself together; you look like hell."

"Charles," Bradley interrupted. "This isn't the time to be down on him."

"Of course, our savior Bradley won't allow anyone to speak the truth. He believes in taking the easy road and acting like there's nothing wrong." Chuckling, he turned to Ken and said, "Face it, the boy is messed up, and he's beyond help."

"That's enough, Charles," Bradley said sharply.

Ken sat up as straight as he could when he heard the tone in Bradley's voice. Everyone knew that Bradley was the toughest of them all, and neither of the other brothers dared to challenge him. He wasn't only the captain of his high school and college football teams, but he was also a third-degree black belt in Taekwondo.

"I'm going to take a shower and have a nap," said Charles. "Call me when it's dinner time."

"You can put your shower on hold," said Bradley, "We're all going fishing now so we can be back before dark and get this dinner started. Tonight, we're going to act like a family, even if I have to tie both of you to a chair and make you sit there all night."

They all looked at one another and burst into laughter. This was something their father would say to them when the three of them got into trouble.

"All right, little brother. Let's go," Charles said, still laughing.

"I need a few minutes," Ken said. "I have to go to the bathroom. I don't feel so good."

"Okay, we'll wait for you but don't take too long," said Bradley. "The fresh air will do you some good. Man, you sure do need it."

Looking sadly at Bradley, Ken rushed to the bathroom, probably to relieve his stomach of all the toxins he drank the night before. Bradley and Charles looked at each other concernedly.

"Well, what do you know, we both agree on something," Bradley said, shrugging his shoulders.

Bradley walked past Charles to get the bait and tackle box from the mudroom, leaving his brother alone to reflect on his comments. He wondered what was really going on with Ken. Remorsefully, he thought he hadn't lived up to the expectations his grandfather had for him. Charles was the oldest, but he was meant to be the glue that held their now much smaller family, together.

Ken stumbled out of the hall bath and walked towards them, holding onto the wall. Charles rushed to help him but was quickly pushed away by his intoxicated brother. Ken looked up at Charles with an expression of vulnerability and frustration all rolled into one. Charles pulled back, and Bradley saw Ken's pain reflected in Charles' eyes. He felt the sorrow and loneliness coming off them in waves. It had been so long since he'd felt connected to his brothers, and now with his grandfather gone, he didn't know how to handle Ken's situation.

"You guys ready?" Bradley asked. "Let's get going before it gets too dark."

"I'm coming, man," replied Ken, as he walked past Charles with his head down.

The three brothers packed their fishing gear and walked down to the lake, each wondering how they had gotten to this point in their lives where their bond was all but broken. The fear of not knowing if they could reweave those family threads was so deep in the atmosphere, only the peace of God could restore their relationship.

***

Sharon and Kera were in the conference room after closing a lucrative deal with a boutique hotel, wanting to not only revamp their current hotel but design the interior of their newest property, set to open the summer of next year. Kera reminded Sharon about the wedding rehearsal on Saturday.

"You know I wouldn't miss it for nothing in the world," exclaimed Sharon. "I'm still in awe that you and Gregg are getting married next week. Heaven put the two of you together."

"What about you and Bradley?" asked Kera.

"What about us? There isn't any history between Bradley and me, like there's with you and Gregg," replied Sharon.

"Maybe not, but everyone and their momma can see there's something special happening between you two. It's just a matter of time before you become Mrs. Bradley DuPont."

"We're just friends. Besides, he doesn't seem as though he's ready for that kind of commitment."

"Why do you think that? The man is gorgeous, intelligent, and has taken a strong liking to you," Kera stated, smiling. "I mean, what is the problem? Don't let one man dictate to you how all men are. You'll miss your blessing and become one of those disgruntled women who has a complex about men and relationships. You know, the ones who sit at home every night alone, with a drink in one hand and watching love stories on the Hallmark Channel, saying, 'Lord, send me a man who will love me like that.' See where the road takes you. You may be surprised with what you end up with."

She knew all too well what her friend was telling her. She too had spent many evenings doing that exact thing. The words of encouragement from her friend made her consider her fear of her own judgement. That made her realize she needed to see where things could go between her and Bradley.

The office phone rang, and Kera answered the call.

"Hello, Catherine. Is everything okay?"

Sharon leaned in towards Kera, curious to know what the client could have wanted. It had only been an hour since the meeting ended, and everything had seemed to go well.

"You want to meet on Saturday? Saturday afternoon is my wedding rehearsal. I'm getting married next week. Is it possible for us to meet on Saturday morning, say around nine a.m.?" Sharon, feeling anxious, was about to fall at the seams, hoping that Catherine didn't change her mind about hiring them.

"Why, thank you. I appreciate that very much. You don't have to get me anything. As a matter of fact, it would give me great pleasure to have you come as my special guest if you can make it. The wedding is on Sunday afternoon. I can email you the details," Kera stated.

"That would be awesome! We look forward to seeing you on Saturday morning at nine sharp. Enjoy the rest of your day!" Kera ended the call with a big smile on her face.

"What did Catherine want?" asked Sharon.

"She said that she's going out of town on Tuesday and would like for us to come to look at the house, so we could get a feel for what needed to be done," explained Kera.

"Okay, that sounds great! That leaves us with two days to prepare and make sure we have everything in order."

Just then, a message popped up on Sharon's cell phone. Immediately, a smile came across her face.

"Is that Mr. DuPont?" asked Kera. "You know I want to know."

Sharon picked up her phone with an eager grin on her face. She couldn't hide it. Every time she got a message from Bradley, it would stir up a feeling in her like no other. Flashbacks of how he'd placed his hands upon her face and put a warm kiss on her lips sent chills down her spine. Sharon cleared her throat so that her words could come out precisely.

"What makes you think it's Bradley texting me? I know other men besides him, you know."

"I'm not crazy," said Kera. "With a man like Bradley, I would smile too. Besides, I enjoy seeing you in such a joyous mood when you speak of him." Kera leaned in towards her. "I'm waiting to hear what the text said. Don't keep me in suspense. Sisters don't hide things from each other."

"I'm not hiding anything from you. There's really nothing to tell. We talk on the phone. I really enjoy talking with him. He makes me feel like he listens to me and understands what I'm about. I just don't want to move too fast with him and then later find out things about him that will hurt me in the long term. I'm not ready for that kind of disappointment," Sharon stated.

"All I know is a man like Bradley only comes once in a lifetime. Don't allow your past to dictate your future. Just give it a try. You never know what can happen. Gregg speaks very highly of him, and I trust my man when he says Bradley is a very good man. I believe he would be a tremendous change for the better in your life; you just have to believe that you're as good for him as I do."

"I know what you're saying, and I promise to give him a try," said Sharon. "That's all I'm promising."

"Listen, Gregg and I are going to have wings and pizza and watch a movie tonight. Want to come?"

"Maybe another time."

"Please tell me you have a legitimate reason for turning down wings and pizza. You better not be ditching me to do work."

As Sharon took in a deep breath, she responded, "No... not this time. I have a date."

Kera jumped up with gladness, gave her friend a big hug, and said, "Girl, I wish I could be a piece of furniture in your house. Oh wait, no, you and Bradley might be doing something I don't need to see."

"You're just as crazy as Aunt Patsi." They both burst out laughing.

"While you're joking, you might learn something from Aunt Patsi. You know she knows how to make a man marry her. She's seen the church altar three times."

"She's the reason Gregg asked me for my hand in marriage. I had to do something to speed up the process, since he was moving as slow as a June bug." Kera rolled her eyes. "Well, I have to get ready for my fiancé and make sure everything is ready for our movie date tonight. I know you're going to have fun as well with Mr. DuPont." Kera gave her a sneaky smile.

"Have a good evening, girl," said Sharon. "We'll talk in the morning."

"If you can't make it in tomorrow, believe me, I won't be mad at you." Kera laughed.

"I'll be here. You can count on it," Sharon replied.

Chapter Twelve

THE BROTHERS RETURNED FROM their fishing trip early because it started raining heavily. They had caught so many fish, the haul would last them for several days. Each one of them looked at the other, not knowing what to say.

Ken walked into the den. Bradley watched as his brother's eyes surveyed the room, landing on each of them before moving to the game table where he found the Monopoly game and burst into laughter. Bradley met Charles' eyes briefly before Ken came into his brother's view. Then watched as a grin took over Charles' face when their little brother raised the Monopoly game in one hand and his other hand on his abdomen, because he was laughing with such intensity, they couldn't help but join in. Memories of them playing the game as children surfaced in their minds.

"Do you remember how to play, old man?" asked Bradley.

"Do you remember how to cheat?" asked Charles.

Bradley looked at Charles, who then looked at Ken and told him to set up the game.

Ken laid out all the cards and pieces as meticulous as he had aways done. He even lined up all of the avatars in a line and counted down to the second when they could claim them.

Bradley snatched his up, watching as Charles and Ken did the same, and was happy to see that none of them went after the same piece. That was the last easy part of the game. The DuPont brothers were incredibly competitive, and winning was equally important to them all.

The three brothers laughed and played like old times. It was as though time stood still and allowed them to get to the place where nothing else mattered but the three of them.

"What happened to us?" Ken asked, his head hanging low as if he was ashamed of how his life turned out.

Silence hit the room like lightning across the sky.

"I'm not sure," replied Charles. "I guess for me, I felt like the two of you were so close, you didn't need me anymore. I went off to college, and every time I came home, you were off having fun together. I felt left out."

"That's not how we saw it," said Bradley. "We felt like you didn't need us since you were doing your thing with your new friends. We didn't want to dampen your image by having your little brothers hanging around you all the time."

"Nothing could be further from the truth. You guys were my best friends. I had so much to tell you about my experiences in college. There were so many times I picked up the phone to call either of you, but I let my pride stop me. As time went on, and I received no call from either of you, it became easier to bury myself in my career so I could forget the pain I felt of having lost my friendship with the two of you."

"I called you that night," Ken said, looking at Charles.

"Ken, what are you talking about?" Charles asked.

"That night I got off from work early. I was so happy, you know? I left my job, came home, and there was my girl, in bed with my co-worker, who asked if I could work in his place that night. I lost it, man. I couldn't help myself. I pounded the guy repeatedly with my fist until he was unconscious. I thought I'd killed him for sure. I turned to her, and she screamed at me like she wasn't the cause of it all. I pushed past her and ran out to a bar and got as drunk as I could. I tried calling you, but you didn't answer. When the cops found me, I didn't even remember what had happened. I was drunk, confused, angry, and hurt.

"All I could see was my girl, having sex with this man I worked with. I thought she and I were heading in the right direction, but she got me, man. She got me." Ken held his head in his hands, breathing heavy for a moment. The tension in the room became thick.

"She took his side and left me out to dry. I don't understand. After all I did for her. After all I gave up for her to make sure she was well taken care of. She didn't want for anything, and she did me like that. If it weren't for Bradley bailing me out, I don't know what I would have done. I left that man with a broken arm, a concussion, and two cracked ribs." Ken shook his head. "I'm still messed up behind that. I can't get a decent job. My life is over."

"Not so, brother," Charles said before taking a breath. "I'm sorry, man. I could say I was busy, but that's a copout. I should have answered my phone or at least called you back, but like I said, I was wrapped up in my pain. So wrapped up in my pain, I wouldn't have had any room for yours. I'm sorry, man. Please forgive me. Both of you, please forgive me." Tears rolled down his cheeks. "I let jealousy and selfishness get in the way of what we had. I should have known better. I know Mom and Dad are rolling over in their graves, and now, Gramps." Charles sobbed incessantly.

"It's okay. All that matters now is that we're here together, and we stay connected. This is what Gramps wanted for us. That's what he said to me before he transitioned. I know that he and our parents are happy now." The three brothers hugged, and Bradley felt the void in his heart where his brothers once were, begin to mend.

***

Daybreak approached, and Bradley woke up early. In just a few hours, they would be saying their final goodbyes to the man who taught them so much about life and being men of integrity. He knew that no one could ever take Gramps' place. Tears rolled down his face as he remembered what a good man his grandfather was.

As he reminisced, Bradley received a text that read,

876-983-7645:I'm sorry for your loss. I'll always be here for you. I love you. I want to see you.

Immediately, his contentment and peace drained away. He tried to school his features when he heard his brother's footfalls but knew he failed when Charles addressed him.

"Is everything okay, little brother? It looks as if you just received some bad news."

"No, I'm good. Just something I thought I left behind in California."

"Talk to me," said Charles, coming around and sitting on the couch across from him, concern in his voice. "I know I haven't been there for either of you, but I can be very useful. After last night, I feel the need to make up for some of the times I've let you both down. I'm a lawyer, you know, but if you need a ride or die partner, I can be that for you too," Charles said, raising an eyebrow.

Bradley's ire and disgust lessened with his brother's attempt at humor. "I don't think it will be a problem."

"Well, if you need me, let me know. I have a team ready to help me with anything I need, day or night, and you don't need to worry about the cost. I've got you taken care of."

Bradley looked gratefully at his brother. "Thanks, man. I really appreciate it."

He sat back for a moment, content and at peace around his big brother for the first time in years. He wondered what Charles would think of Sharon. The thought had just formed when another one came swiftly on its heels Sharon. She was hoping he would come over. He glanced at his watch. It was too late now. He considered calling her but once again, it was late. He decided to text her a brief message of apology hoping she would understand.

Bradley: Are you awake?

Bradley waited five minutes and when there was no return text or bubbles showing the intent of a text he assumed Sharon had fallen asleep.

Bradley: I'm sorry my night went so late. It would have been nice to see you. I hope I get to see you tomorrow at some point.

Bradley took a breath with his finger hovering over the send button.

Bradley: Goodnight, Sweetheart.

Chapter Thirteen

GREGG AND KERA WERE getting ready for the funeral service when Gregg noticed Kera wasn't her usual free-spirited self.

"What's wrong with you, baby?"

"I don't know." She sighed. "Remember, I told you about the new client we were going to meet with yesterday?"

"Yes," replied Gregg.

"We met with her, and everything went exceptionally well."

"So, why the doom and gloom look?" he asked.

"She seems really nice, but there's something not right about her. She and her son are relocating here from the West so she can be closer to her fiancé, who is her son's father. Her demeanor and the way she expressed herself when she spoke of her fiancé was just weird. I can't figure it out, but it's something."

"Okay, Detective Prescott, slow down on the suspicions. Could she just be awkward around new people?" suggested Gregg.

Kera pulled a face as she thought it over. "I don't know. Catherine Morris doesn't strike me as an awkward person."

"Did you say Catherine Morris?" asked Gregg.

"Yes... why? Do you know her?" She continued fixing her hair and makeup.

"Baby, where did you say she's from?" asked Gregg

"The West. California, I believe." Kera's eyes lit up as she answered Gregg's question. She could feel the hair on her arms rise up as chills moved over her skin.

"Oh, my goodness," he exclaimed, shaking his head.

There's no way this could be the same Catherine Morris. He wanted to quickly reassure her that she had nothing to worry about. "It may just be a coincidence. There are plenty of people with that name in the world." Gregg pressed his hand against his chin.

"You do know her. What are you not telling me, Gregg Wilson? Tell me!"

"I knew a Catherine Morris back in college, but she graduated, and I thought she moved to Italy for a job. She was not, shall I say, a good girl. Anyway, it's been some years but last I heard, she was still there. There could have been a child by now. Maybe it's just a coincidence. Now that I think about it, Catherine Morris does sound like it could be a popular name. I'm sure there's nothing for you to worry about."

The Catherine he'd known was a woman driven by ambition, determined to reach the pinnacle of success. Her demeanor exuded beauty and allure, yet beneath it lay a steely resolve. Crossing her was just something people didn't do because she was known to stop at nothing to eliminate any perceived competition. She had graduated at the top of her class with a finance degree, and garnered favor from professors and peers alike, her capabilities evident to all who knew her.

"You might be right. This Catherine Morris only has one child... a son."

Gregg stood in front of her and slid his arms around her waist.

"You're the woman for me, so I'm not concerned about this Catherine person. When I open my eyes, your beautiful face is the only one I see, and when I close my eyes, it is the only one I want to remember," said Gregg. Then he pulled her close and kissed her.

He knew deep down inside he had to do some investigation of his own. Even as he reassured his fiancée that she had nothing to be concerned about, he knew he had to be sure himself.

***

Sharon phoned Kera to let her know that she would be bringing Aunt Patsi to the funeral because her chauffeur had the day off, and Sharon only lived ten minutes from her. Sharon knew that this would be a ride she wouldn't soon forget.

Aunt Patsi was waiting by the stoop in a sleek green, sleeveless ruched bodycon dress with an asymmetrical hemline. She had clearly been waiting for Sharon to arrive. She threw her purse on her arm, so anxious to get going, she practically ran down the three steps to her driveway. As soon as Patsi got in the car, she started in on Sharon, asking several questions about her personal life.

"My personal business is just that!" Sharon's eyes lowered. She felt as if she was being quizzed on a dating show in front of millions of viewers.

"Honey, I know you think I'm not in my right mind and that I don't have any sense when I'm talking," she stated.

"Aunt Patsi, what do you mean? I never said that about you."

"You don't have to. My family thinks that way, and it shows when I walk into a room," she stated.

Sharon couldn't help noticing the sadness in her voice and when Aunt Patsi didn't say any more, Sharon didn't feel the need to press her. The day would be hard enough as it was. She and Aunt Patsi would have more opportunities to talk. She would even create a few if she had to.

***

The church was packed. People from all over the country had come to say farewell to the man who had made such a positive impact in the community and beyond. Guest after guest rose up to say something about the difference he'd made in their lives. Hearing all of the kind words people said about him made Sharon feel sad, but also happy that she had an opportunity to meet the man. It also gave her a sense of the type of man Bradley was.

He and his brothers sat in the front row as the pastor preached the eulogy. Sharon wanted so desperately to go to him and hold him and make him understand how much she would be there for him.

She felt the vibration of her phone buzzing in her purse. Although she tried to ignore it, curiosity got the better of her, and she had to know just who it was. Finally, she reached into her purse to take a quick peek. Aunt Patsi, who sat next to her, made no hesitation to look on also. Sharon tried to keep her phone from being noticed, but her aunt wasn't surprised when she'd seen the name of the person on the telephone screen. As she opened the text message, it read,

Bradley: Sorry about last night. Did you get my text?

Sharon: Yes. I was asleep by the time you sent it and with knowing what today was, I thought I would wait to respond.

Bradley: Thank you for being so understanding.

Sharon: You're welcome.

Bradley: May I come over later? I really want to spend some time with you.

Sharon: Yes.

Bradley: Okay. See you around 6 p.m.

Sharon: Okay

After catching the quick glimpse of the exchange of texts, Aunt Patsi could hardly contain herself.

She decided to put her two cents in and leaned over to murmur to Sharon, "If I were you, I wouldn't waste any time getting him. He's a good man, just like his grandfather was." She wiggled her eyebrows at Sharon, but the woman didn't seem to take the hint. Sharon only looked at her in surprise, smiled, and turned her attention towards the front of the church.

The seasoned woman knew all too well about letting a good man get away. She remembered how she had fallen in love with one man who had stolen her heart many years ago, and how she let her career take precedence over their relationship, only to lose him in her absence. When she returned to reclaim him, she found he had given his heart to another woman. She still couldn't forget him, and she'd had to live with her choices ever since.

Tears rolled down her cheeks. This was the last time she would see the man she loved. Ronald DuPont was the only man who could make her happy, and now he was gone forever. The wounds she felt in her heart were too much for her to bear.

"May I borrow the keys to the car? I just need some quiet space."

She sensed Sharon watching her, but the woman didn't say anything. She just dug in her purse and passed the keys, to which Patsi was grateful. She gave Sharon a wan smile, then got up quickly and walked out of the church. Trying not to make a sound, she exited the church with a face full of tears.

***

Kera's mom Sara and a few other women from the church in the bereavement ministry left immediately after the funeral and headed over to the ranch to prepare for the guests who would arrive there.

Sharon knew they would need some help if even half of the crowd from the church descended upon the ranch so instead of waiting in line with all of those wanting shake hands and give Bradley and his brothers a few words of encouragement, she went straight to the car. She knew she would see Bradley at the repast as well as later on that evening.

She was also concerned about Aunt Patsi and her hasty retreat from the service. When she got in the car, Patsi's appearance and demeanor had improved. Though her eyes were still red, it looked like she had reapplied her makeup.

"Are you okay?" Sharon asked, then wanted to put her palm to her forehead. Of course, the woman wasn't all right. "Do you want to talk about it while we drive to the repast? Do you still want to go to the repast?" She opened her mouth again but forced herself to stop bombarding the woman with questions until she at least answered one.

Aunt Patsi turned towards her. "I still intend to go to the repast. Did you see all those people in that church? Sara wouldn't have a chance with just her small crew."

Sharon smiled at her softly, then started the car. "Will you be okay?" she asked before putting the car in gear.

Patsi nodded, and Sharon pulled out of the parking space and followed a small line of cars out of the parking lot. She was happy again that she hadn't hesitated in getting to her car.

She was on the road before Patsi spoke again. "Don't waste time trying to figure out the hows of life. Just have the courage and faith to believe that no matter what, it will all work out for the best. All you have is hope, and once that's gone, there's really nothing left."

"Okay, that was really deep," said Sharon. "Are you going to be all right?" Patsi was in another world as she gazed out the window with folded hands across her lap. When she turned back to her, Sharon recognized the expression of sadness and regret.

"Of course, I'm all right. I'm saying to you that if you want this man, you must leave the ugly past where it belongs. Make sure you don't let it back in, or you'll always have regrets. The future doesn't have room for the past, so let it go. Real love, like life, is just a vapor, and in one blow of the wind, it can pass you by and go on to someone else. Someone who is ready to receive what you're too afraid to accept. I know, I've been there."

Those words went so deep into Sharon's soul, that it made her think about her choices when it came to Bradley. She wondered if it was possible to open herself up to receive real love, if that's what Bradley was offering, or let fear keep her bound because of her last relationship? Sharon didn't want to end up like Aunt Patsi, who in her late fifties was holding onto wishes that seemed to never come true.

Patsi was known for having a good time and being pretty free with men, but Sharon had thought it was just Patsi's lively and willful spirit. Her way of controlling the narrative of her life.

Now, she wondered if it was more because Aunt Patsi was trying to fill an emptiness in her life. An emptiness Sharon knew couldn't be filled with just physical pleasure.

A long, hard look at reality, and the wisdom from this unlikely source, made Sharon think about her future happiness. She'd never given any thought to it like that before, but she knew she had to do something quickly.

Chapter Fourteen

When Bradley and his brothers returned to Gramps' house from the funeral, friends and family warmly greeted them. Kera and Gregg arrived shortly after, but Sharon was nowhere to be seen.

Was she in another part of the house?

With so many people walking around him and blocking his way, he grew more impatient by the minute. His search was momentarily interrupted when he entered the kitchen to find Sara and some of the other women preparing the food for everyone.

"Hi, baby," Sara said as she walked around the island to hug him. "Where are your brothers?"

"They're in the living room, mixing with the guests."

Sara stood back to look at him. "I know this is a stupid question, but I'm going to ask anyway. How are you guys holding up?"

"We're good, Mrs. Sara. It's just going to take some time to adjust to Gramps not being here. I think we're going to be all right."

"Just know that if there's anything you need, you can call me. You know we got you."

"I know, Mrs. Sara. We appreciate that."

"Well, I made food for you all for the week, and I've already put it up for you in the refrigerator, so all you need to do is put it in the microwave and heat it up." She beckoned for him to follow her to the pantry and pointed to the top shelf. "I made your favorite lemon sour cream pound cake and a Sprite upside-down cake as well."

Rubbing his hands together in excitement, he thanked her and gave her a hug. As they closed the door to the pantry, he turned to see a familiar face at the other end of the vast kitchen. One he had been waiting to see all day. It was her. She was finally here. His heart leaped, and a big smile came across his face.

Aunt Patsi stood beside her, and Sharon knew she took notice of everything. She knew she had to help Sharon understand that if she missed out on this opportunity with Bradley, she would regret it for the rest of her life and she didn't want that for her.

Chuckling, Patsi pushed her gently forward, whispering in her ear, "Go over and talk to him. If you don't, I might make my move on him instead. You know young men love older women. I might be the one to rock his world, honey."

Sharon looked at her with a little hesitation and whispered back as quietly as possible "I don't want to come off as being desperate. Besides, this isn't the right place for me to be thinking about that with him. He's grieving."

"That's why you should take advantage of this chance. Look at him, he needs someone to comfort him and hold him and tell him that they're here for him... If you don't, then I'll go since you're too scared to tell him how you feel." Suddenly, she pretended to brush past Sharon to go over to Bradley.

Sharon grabbed her by the elbow and said, "Okay, okay... I'll go."

"It's about time. Be sexy with it. Men love that in a woman." Aunt Patsi smiled enthusiastically.

Sharon walked through the crowded kitchen. There were so many people gathered around him, she had to talk herself into moving forward. She looked back at Aunt Patsi, who silently cheered her on with the nodding of her head. Then she stood in front of Bradley, locking eyes with him. There was no need for words. The attraction could be seen between the two of them.

"Hello," she said. She tried hard not let on that her feelings for him had grown deeper than she had shown. She held out her hand for him to shake as if this were the first time they had met.

"Hello," he said. He took her hand in his and placed them to her side before pulling her into a warm embrace. "I'm so glad to see you. I was beginning to think I wouldn't get to see your beautiful face before this evening."

She smiled and was about to reply when she was interrupted. "Well, well, little brother, who is this ray of sunshine?" Immediately, they both turned to face him.

"Charles, please meet Sharon. Sharon, this is my older brother Charles," said Bradley.

"Nice to meet you," said Sharon.

"No, the pleasure is all mine. It's nice to see my brother smiling again," replied Charles.

"I'm guessing she's why I haven't been able to find you for the last ten minutes. There's someone here to see you, Bradley," Charles said before looking back at Sharon and addressing her again. "I'll make sure he comes back to you in just a few minutes."

Bradley whispered in her ear, "Would you please meet me at the veranda in five minutes? There's something I would like to talk to you about."

Sharon wondered what he wanted to talk with her about. He seemed anxious to be alone with her. "Okay," she said.

"She's in the study waiting for you," said Charles.

"She... do you know who she is and what she wants?" Bradley asked.

"No, she wouldn't say, except that you two were old friends."

Sharon's stomach immediately turned flips when she heard these words. A familiar feeling of unease came over her. Instead, she calmed her emotions. Maybe this woman was purely innocent, and there was no cause for worry. They were at a repast after all.

"Okay, I'll be back. Don't forget what I said," he told Sharon.

She looked long and hard at Bradley as he left the kitchen, wondering what was going on and why there was such urgency. Trying hard not let her imagination get the better of her, she took a sip of her punch and decided to ask him later. She would see him in a few minutes, after all.

Bradley walked out of the kitchen to meet the mysterious woman in his grandfather's study.

Who could it be? What could she want with me?

Aunt Patsi made her way over to Sharon to start her own investigation.

"What was that about?" she asked.

"I don't know," said Sharon. She was just as curious as Aunt Patsi.

"Well, don't you think you should go find out and make sure it's not someone you need to be concerned about? Standing here beating yourself up with suspense won't help the situation."

"I'm sure it's nothing, Aunt Patsi. It's probably something to do with his grandfather."

"Huh, yeah right! Either you're the most trustworthy person I've ever known, or you're the stupidest woman in this world. I saw this woman that he's going in there to meet, and baby, she's not here for his grandfather. Besides, one man is dead and can't do a thing for her, but your man is alive and well and can do whatever she wishes. Go take a look if you don't believe me."

Sharon looked at her aunt in confusion, but she knew deep down that if Aunt Patsi said something, it was true. No matter how much she had to drink, she wasn't a woman who would lie. She had no choice but to listen. Patsi would never give up until she did. She followed her out of the kitchen, not only to appease her but also for her own curiosity.

"Come, let's mix a little while we walk towards the office and take a peek in. I'll lead the way," said Patsi.

Chapter Fifteen

As they approached the office, she heard arguing, which became louder the closer they got. Sharon stopped abruptly and stood close by the door to listen in on the conversation.

"Why are you here right now, when I just buried my grandfather?" asked Bradley. "I told you I never wanted to see you again."

"I tried telling you, but you kept hanging up on me. What was I supposed to do? You never gave me closure. You left me all alone, and I had no one to turn to. I miss you, baby," said the sobbing woman.

Sharon felt uneasiness in her spirit as she listened to the conversation. Aunt Patsi took her hand. It was obvious from the tone of the voices that bounced off the walls, that this wasn't two mere acquaintances having an argument; it was much deeper than that.

"Let's just wait. There has to be a logical explanation," Aunt Patsi said.

"That woman's voice sounds so familiar. I think I know her," Sharon stated.

"Are you sure, baby?"

The room went silent, and Sharon couldn't help but peek through the small crack in the door they'd left ajar, to see what was going on. As she turned towards the door to look in, sadness washed through her at the recognition of the woman pleading with Bradley. She felt like an idiot as she watched the woman place her hands on Bradley's chest and lift up on her toes to bring their faces together. She closed and moved away from the door, unable to watch another woman kiss the man she'd... she'd... She was such a fool.

Emotions consumed Sharon, but there were so many, she had trouble figuring out which one dominated the others. She had a flashback to when she discovered Mark's infidelity, and she berated herself for her continual bad judgment. She couldn't believe what she had seen. She was hurt, and she knew it showed. She marched past the crowd to find the bathroom, so she could compose herself before leaving the house. At this point, she was unable to hold back the tears that ran down her cheeks.

She knew that it made no sense. Why was her reaction to this betrayal so strong? It had only been days since she'd met Bradley. She knew even as she asked herself the questions. Sure, it had been days, but it was also the physical and emotional connection. It had been the ease in which they were able to share about their lives as well as the hope she'd put into those days for something real and lasting that she now mourned.

When she finally composed herself enough to get through the throng of well-wishers without drawing attention, she came out of the bathroom, and Aunt Patsi was there.

She cupped Sharon's cheek, and it was all Sharon could do to keep from bursting out crying. Sharon took her hand away but held it in hers.

"Go on, baby girl. I got you. Do you want to talk to him? See if what we heard is true?"

Sharon shook her head, knowing she couldn't be calm enough to seek any answers rationally.

"Okay. You go. I'm sure I can get a ride from Sara or one of the others in the kitchen."

"You sure?" was all Sharon could get out.

"Yes, sweety."

Sharon took a deep breath and hugged Patsi quickly. "Thank you," she said before making her way through the crowd back to the kitchen to get her purse and leave.

Aunt Patsi was going to read the two in the study the riot act. She had in her mind that she would tear them apart for hurting poor Sharon. She stood in front of the doorway and cleared her throat to let them know they had been caught. With her arms folded and her feet padding the hardwood floor, she got their attention.

"What in the heaven is going on in here?" she asked. Before either of them could say anything, she continued, "I see you're trying to play my niece, and your real slick at it, too. You bring the other woman to the house on the day of your grandfather's funeral. Of all the old, dirty tricks in the world. I ought to take off my shoes and beat you down like a rabid dog."

"What? It's not what it looks like, Aunt Patsi," Bradley began.

"Patsi knows exactly what it looks like. You can't play that stuff with me, I know better!"

"Who is this old biddy, Bradley?" asked the woman.

"Old biddy... little girl, if I were you, I would shut my mouth before you need a dentist. You don't know me, and I guarantee you that you don't want any of this." Aunt Patsi pointed at herself. "This old biddy will make you wish you had more respect for your elders... looking like you just came in from a hoochie meeting."

The confrontation in the study was loud enough to carry, so Aunt Patsi wasn't surprised when Gregg and Kera arrived at the threshold of the study.

"Catherine, what are you doing here? I didn't know you knew the DuPonts." Kera gasped.

Aunt Pasti watched the smug smile take over Catherine's face, and she knew she was lying. "Yes, this is my fiancé."

"That's it, Catherine," Bradley said. "You've caused enough problems already! You need to leave."

She watched as Kera opened and closed her mouth with everything from disbelief to confusion, then anger took over her features. She couldn't believe what she was hearing. She meditated a bit on the words spoken, and a river of questions flooded through her mind.

"I don't believe what I'm hearing," Kera said. "Bradley, this is our client. We didn't even know you two knew each other, let alone that you were engaged."

Kera looked around the room, and Patsi followed her gaze then registered a deep unease in her stance. "Oh, my goodness, Sharon," Kera said to herself before looking at Gregg.

"Did you know about this?"

"Baby, as I told you earlier, I knew Catherine from a long time ago, but I didn't know this. Besides, it wouldn't be my place to say anything. This has nothing to do with us. It's between them," he said, pointing at Bradley. "Bradley is a grown man who knows how to handle his business."

"That may be true, but if you knew anything, you should have told me. My business is involved, and Sharon. Sharon has been through a lot, and you know this. You should have told me, Gregg. No secrets... remember?"

"Hey." He pulled Kera towards him and gently held her. "I'm just as upset as you are, but this isn't our battle. They'll have to work this out on their own, without us interfering. We can only offer them support and nothing more. Besides, Sharon is a big, strong girl."

He looked at his friend with disappointment in his eyes.

"Is this true? Are you engaged?" asked Ken.

"We're not. That was over more than three years ago, and she knows why." He looked at the woman next to him up and down with a scowl. "So, Catherine, you need to stop referring to me as your fiancé; we've been over for a long time. I don't have time for this. I need to find Sharon right now."

"She just left. And with good reason," Aunt Patsi said, watching him carefully. She was pleased to see the distress on his face morph into panic just before he walked swiftly out of the room.

"I'll call her," said Kera as she pressed numbers on her phone, then placed it to her ear. After a few moments, she turned to Gregg again. "Baby, she's not answering. I'm going over to her place to make sure she's all right."

"Okay. Let me know when you've spoken with her. I'm going to stay here with Bradley to find out what's going on."

"He just left. You may want to follow him," said Patsi, barely giving them a glance as she turned to the woman who had caused all the drama and made her girl cry.

Gregg and Kera ran out of the room.

"Speaking of leaving, don't you think you should be getting your-self up out of here? Seems you've overstayed your welcome, Miss Thang," said Aunt Patsi.

She walked up to Catherine, feeling murderous, but she could sense they had an audience.

The woman's eyes widened at what she saw in Patsi's eyes.

"I have every right to be here," the woman said, lifting her chin in defiance.

Patsi shrugged. "And I have every right to drag you out of what should be a peaceful time of reflection and bereavement for Mr. DuPont's boys. How would you like to leave?" Those who knew Aunt Patsi and her reputation looked on in fascination. They all knew Aunt Patsi was a fiery woman and wasn't one to mess with. One thing was for certain, she didn't play when it came down to family and those she cared about.

Chapter Sixteen

SHARON DROVE OUT TO Lake Murray to compose herself. This was her own private getaway from everything and everyone. The air was still, and a nice breeze came up off the water as she gazed into the night light. Out on the lake, she could see a boat in the distance. She watched as the waves slowly rocked it back and forth. She thought about how much of her life had been just like the motions of that boat going forward, only to be pulled back into the same situation. Those dreaded feelings of hurt, shame, and disgust overtook her again. She probably didn't have any right to be driving, as messed up as she was. All the emotions she felt in the past came up, and she couldn't stop crying and shaking. It would be a long while before she could wrap her mind around driving back anywhere.

How could he do this to me? No. How could I've been so stupid to think this could work, that he could possibly be the man for me? Boaz? There's no such thing as Boaz. I'm done with relationships; maybe I should leave and start a new life.

Sharon sat in her car for hours, going back over the past week, the past months and years and vowed to make a change. and planning out her life without Bradley; without men.

***

Kera and Gregg arrived at Sharon's to find Bradley sitting on her front porch. Kera watched as Bradley slowly released his grip from his face and rise from his spot on the top step. Once they got close enough, she noticed his red-rimmed eyes. Her heart lurched at his expression of expectation that turned to disappointment when he didn't find who he was looking for behind her and Gregg.

She let Gregg walk ahead of her, not knowing what to expect from this wounded man.

Gregg placed his hand on Bradley's shoulder. "Are you okay?" Gregg asked.

"I messed up big time, Gregg. I should have answered her calls. I knew how persistent she could be, but I hadn't spoken to her in years. I still don't know what she wanted, coming all this way, today of all days. I just know that I have to find Sharon. Tell her she has no reason to... That I... That—" He took a deep breath, and his shoulders fell.

"We were supposed to talk." He blew out a ragged breath. "...so that I could tell her, but then everything happened so fast. I never felt anything like this for any woman in my life. What am I going to do? I can't lose her, man."

"Is there something you haven't told me about Catherine?"

Bradley shook his head. "No. No, man."

Kera looked at Gregg, who shook his head. "I don't know, man, but if it's meant to be, I know you'll find a way to make her see that."

Kera took that moment to walk up the steps to her friend's home. She removed the spare key she had to Sharon's house from her purse and unlocked the front door. She entered the house, calling out Sharon's name, hoping she was either in the shower or taking a nap, but she received no answer. She went upstairs to see if she was in her bedroom, but the entire house was silent. She met Gregg back in the hallway. "No car in the garage."

"Where could she be? I don't understand. It's not like her to not answer her phone when I call. This isn't good, Gregg. We have to find her!"

"I'm sorry, Kera. I didn't mean to hurt her. I would never hurt her. You have to believe me," Bradley pleaded.

She saw that he really meant it and felt sympathy for him. "I know, Bradley. Right now, we just need to concentrate on finding her."

"You're right. Thank you for not judging me."

"It's not for me to judge. You're both our friends, and whatever you need to do to fix this, we'll help you do it," said Kera.

They discussed and dismissed all the places Sharon could be. The more time passed, the higher Kera saw Bradley's anxiety grow. He paced, looking agitated by the second.

She didn't know all that had transpired between him and her friend, but it was obvious that he had deep feelings for Sharon. She watched as his shoulders bowed, and her heart went out to him.

"Gregg and I will take a look back around the church and a couple of Sharon and my favorite spots. If we find anything, we'll call you.

Why don't you go back to your house and see if she came back that way."

"Okay," Bradley said.

***

A half hour later, Bradley sat in his car on the fringes of his property, too upset to get close to the crowd of people still in his home.

A slight pain formed at the crown of his head, from the agonizing thought of Sharon not being in his life. The suspense was killing him. He took a moment to reflect on the first time he laid eyes on her at their best friend's engagement party not even a full week ago. The fear of not knowing if they had a future made him a little crazy. He needed to be with her. Bradley prayed quietly, seeking clarity, peace, and asking for a miracle.

His phone rang, interrupting his talk with God. He scrambled to pick it up.

"Hello."

"Hey." Kera's voice came over the line. "We haven't found her yet, but I know she'll show up. Don't worry. Maybe she's driving around and will come home soon. Let's just give her time to calm down, and then we'll contact you in the morning."

Bradley agreed, but he wanted to keep searching for her. He didn't want to let the morning light appear without knowing she was safe, and they would be okay. He never wanted anyone so badly in his life, and he knew she was the one for him. Each passing minute created an agonizing pain in his stomach. He decided to drive by her house again to make sure she hadn't come home while they were out looking for her. Bradley examined the house for any sign of movement, but there was none. He made the decision to go home, hoping he would hear from her soon.

Bradley pulled up to the ranch. Switching the engine off, he leaned back in the car and took a deep breath before getting out. Once in the house, he noticed the light in the family room was on. He knew that one, if not both of his brothers, was awake, and he wasn't ready to give answers to their many questions. All he could do was hope they just forgot to cut the light off. This would at least allow him to miss the Jeopardy questions concerning his personal life. Slowly, he got out and walked into the house. He was immediately greeted by Charles.

"Well, I see I'm not the only one in the family who has female problems," said Charles. Bradley turned to see his brother lying prostrate on the couch with a book in his hands. "Yes, I waited up for you. Just wanted to make sure everything was okay." He held up two fingers. "Scout's honor."

"Look at me, man; I'm a mess right now," said Bradley. He spread his arms as wide as he could.

"Get some rest, and we can talk about it in a few hours. We'll come up with a plan, and we'll get through this. I promise," said Charles.

"Thanks, bro. I'm really glad you guys are here." He looked around for Ken.

"Don't worry; Boy Genius is sound asleep in his room, tucked in and everything." Charles returned to his book with a big smile.

Once Bradley was in his room, he reflected on the way Sharon's face lit up the last time he spoke with her. He also remembered how Aunt Patsi had lit into him.

He just needed to know how much Sharon had heard and seen. He needed to know how to make it right with her. He wasn't willing to give up on the possibility of something good, and if he felt this way after only a few days, he knew it had to be something worth saving.

He got down on his knees to say his prayers. He whispered to God for her protection and for a chance to explain himself.

***

Aunt Patsi had just finished watching a movie and drinking her favorite wine when she heard her doorbell ring. She held onto her house dress, trying to picture who it was. She ran to her drawer in the hallway, to pull out her gun from the box she kept hidden in case of intruders. "Somebody has lost their mind, coming to my house this late. It had better be someone dying, or about to die, coming to my house this time of the night," she said.

As Patsi approached the door, she looked out and noticed it was Sharon. Opening the door, Sharon was at that moment simply a distraught young woman. She had been crying for a while. Her black mascara was swept away from her eyes and running down her cheeks, fading into her skin.

She held out her hand and motioned for her to come inside. "Child, come in. What are you doing out here at this time of night?"

"I didn't want to go home and be alone," Sharon said with her voice trembling.

She shivered from the frigid air coming off the lake. "I'll make a fresh pot of coffee, and we can sit down and talk," Aunt Patsi said as she led her into the living room. "Take the blanket from the sofa and wrap yourself in it to help you warm up while the coffee is brewing."

Sharon made herself comfortable, but by the time Aunt Patsi returned with the coffee, she found Sharon fast asleep.

Patsi prayed softly, "Lord, I know you and I haven't spoken much in a while, and I can sometimes be difficult to handle, but if you'll just forget about me for a moment and give this young lady peace in her spirit like I know you can, I would really appreciate it." She pulled Sharon's shoes off, placed her feet up on the couch, and got another blanket from the hall closet to put over her.

When Patsi was sure of the stillness, presence, and calm from the Lord was palpable, she whispered, "Thank you, Lord." She turned off the light and started towards her bedroom.

"Thank you, Aunt Patsi." Patsi turned towards her with a smile on her face. She thought, *I was once you a lifetime ago, so there's no need for thanks. Someone was there for me, and now it's my turn to help someone else.*

"You're welcome, honey. You just get some rest now, and we'll talk over breakfast in the morning." At last, the two women said good night to each other and went to bed.

Chapter Seventeen

THE SMELL OF BACON and eggs entered Sharon's nose, and her stomach took notice. It had been a long time since she was awakened by the smell of a home-cooked breakfast *and* singing. *Singing?* she wondered to herself. "Oh my, she's singing a song of praise?" Sharon looked around to make sure she hadn't died and gone to heaven. "Nope, I'm still in the land of the living," she whispered.

"Good morning, and yes, you're still in the land of the living. Now, what does that mean, may I ask?" said Aunt Patsi.

"Nothing, I just never heard you sing, let alone a church song. You actually have a beautiful voice. Why is it that you don't sing more often?"

"I chose not to sing in public anymore." Her voice shook as she fought back hurtful tears.

"What do you mean by... anymore? Why is that?" Sharon asked.

"I used to sing in social clubs for a while. That's how I met my first husband. He was a part of an elite social club in Rochester, and I was invited to sing at one of the events. When I finished singing, he came over to where I was standing with a group of friends and introduced himself. He was handsome, funny, and rich. I was young and figured I had finally found someone who understood me."

"So, how long were you two married?"

"Two years, and it was wonderful." She took a deep breath as if it were her last. "He died two weeks after our anniversary of a brain aneurysm. It took me a long time to get over losing him, but I did. Enough about me, tell me, what are you going to do about you and Bradley?"

"I can't believe I allowed myself to be hurt by another man. I never thought I would end up back in the same situation as my last relationship. There has to be something about me that keeps attracting men who want to use me." Sharon summed up some of her thoughts during her time of meditation at her lake. "I consider myself a good judge of character when it comes to people in general. But when it comes to my personal life, I tend to make the worst decisions."

"You know, you can sit here and wallow in your sorrow and feel pity for yourself, or you can pick yourself up and move forward. Life is about decisions, for good or bad. When you see people, you see what they present to you. You have to go somewhere deep inside yourself to find out what you want, and not what you think the other person can do for you."

"Well, I expected more from him. He made me feel things I never thought were possible." Sharon's shoulders shrugged as she looked down at her empty ring finger.

"Were you looking for him to be the man he is, or did you want him to be who you think he should be? You have to make up your mind what you want and how you're going to handle this situation, honey. Don't waste time thinking about what could happen. Make things happen."

Sharon knew that eventually, she would have to face Bradley, and he would want to talk about what happened. Just as she was about to answer, she received a call from the investors in Europe. She had forgotten that they were waiting on her to decide whether to open up an office there. She took a deep breath and tried to sound as excited as she could before answering the call.

"Hello, how are you? Yes, I thought about our last conversation, and it would be an honor to visit. Thank you so much." Sharon turned to Patsi and told her about the call.

"That sounds like a great opportunity." Patsi leaned in and lowered her tone to make sure Sharon was listening closely, "Just make sure you don't leave without speaking to him. You don't want to have any regrets. I made that mistake in the past, and it haunted me for many years."

"Tell me, Aunt Patsi, who were you talking about at the funeral?" Sharon grabbed her cup of coffee, not taking her eyes off Aunt Patsi so that she would catch sight of her waiting on a response.

"Many... many years ago, I was engaged to a man in my senior year of college. He meant the world to me, and I let him get away. It was almost identical to your situation. I left and never told him how much I loved him. I thought when I pursued my dreams, he would always be there when I came home. It didn't work that way. The distance between us was too much, and we slowly drifted apart. After graduation, I was going to make things right with us, but I found out he was engaged and soon to marry another woman. In my despair, I secluded myself from him. I returned home with a broken heart, and it was my fault."

"I'm sorry. May I ask who he was?"

She paused for a moment with such sadness in her wet eyes. "Just know that he was a man I deeply cared about and still do to this day."

"Wow, he must have been an amazing person!"

She nodded with tears streaming down her face. "That's why I encourage you to follow your heart and allow yourself to face your fears head on."

The doorbell rang, pulling them out of their morose thoughts.

"Are you expecting someone?" Sharon asked Patsi.

"Nope."

Sharon sighed. "I guess it's for me then." She took a sip of her coffee to prepare herself for company. If she knew her best friend, and she did, it would be Kera. She steeled herself for the many questions she knew her friend was about to ask regarding her disappearance last night.

Patsi left the room, and it was only a few seconds before she heard the door open and Patsi's motherly tone.

"Good morning. To what do I owe the honor of your visit this early in the morning?"

"Good morning, Aunt Patsi. Mom asked me to bring some of the left-over cake from the ceremony last night. Is that Sharon's car outside? Is she here?"

"Yes, she's in the kitchen, finishing up breakfast."

Kera appeared at the kitchen door not even a full moment later and pulled Sharon into a hug. Patsi trailed in behind her.

"Hey, we were worried about you," said Kera. "You didn't answer my calls. All sorts of thoughts ran through my head. Are you all right?"

"Yes, I'm all right. I just needed to think."

Kera whispered, "What made you come here of all places?"

"She actually helped me get through the night and even fixed me one of the best breakfasts I've had in a long time."

"Really?" Kera looked between Sharon and Aunt Patsi.

Sharon nodded, smiling serenely. Kera smiled back. "I'm glad. I was so worried."

"Sorry about that. I never meant for you to worry about me."

Kera watched her for a minute before nodding and humming.

"You know, Bradley was out looking for you as well. He's really concerned, Sharon. If I hadn't seen it in his eyes, I wouldn't have believed it. I really believe there's more to the story than what we know."

Sharon considered Kera's words for a moment. "I spent half my life waiting for the right relationship and even allowed myself to put up with stuff I never thought I would. All I got in return is a kick in my heart. Kera, I can't take this anymore. I should have seen the signs. I mean, what was I thinking?"

"I know it hurts, and I wish I could take it away."

"I'm going to get dressed and go home. I've thought about the job in Paris, and I think I'm going to see what they have to offer us. I need to get away to help me think more clearly. If I stay here, I'll crazy."

"I think it would be a good idea to put a new perspective on this situation and determine what it is that you want. I think you ought to talk with him and hear his side of the story," said Patsi.

"I don't know what to say, think, or feel. I'm so confused," Sharon whispered, staring down at her hands.

"No one said you had to figure everything out all at once, but you have to face reality. Only you can determine your destiny. You make the choice. We can only give you advice." She walked over to Sharon and gave her a big hug. "You don't want to live a life of regrets. I'm going to leave you two alone. Would you be so kind to lock the door when you leave? I'm going to take a long bubble bath and calm my nerves with a glass of wine." Aunt Patsi turned to walk away but before she took more than two steps, she leaned down to grab the bottle and glass she had left on the coffee table the night before. Holding up the bottle on the way down the hall, Sharon and Kera just watched with dropped jaws.

"This early... Auntie?" asked Kera.

Patsi's laugh came out like music as she walked further down the hall. "It is never too early. If I were still in Paris, I would have finished a whole bottle by now." Kera and Sharon looked at each other and shook their heads. They couldn't help but burst into laughter.

"Girl, I'll check on you later. Please let me know if you need anything. You know Gregg and I have your back."

"I know and thanks for always being here for me."

"You got it."

Chapter Eighteen

SHARON DROVE HOME THAT afternoon feeling overwhelmed by her feelings and what Kera relayed to her about Bradley. She walked into the kitchen and threw her Louis Vuitton purse on the island, then grabbed a wine glass and poured a healthy serving for herself to calm her nerves. While walking into her bedroom, she caught sight of the picture of her parents on the hall wall.

She stared at the photo, wondering how they'd found each other and wished they could tell her how to navigate this part of her life. She removed the photo from the wall and held it close to her heart as she imagined her mom giving the advice that only a mother could give.

"Mom, Dad, I wish you were here. I feel so lonely and scared right now."

The house was quiet, and for a moment, she felt a cool breeze pass her shoulder, with a faint sound she could swear was her mother calling her name.

"*Mommy!*" Her heart sank, and she couldn't suppress her emotions anymore. Sharon cried aloud as the tears rolled down her cheek as she neared the oversized bathtub in her master bathroom.

Sharon ran her bath water and walked back into the bedroom to get something comfortable to lounge in. She got undressed and slowly stepped into the warm bath filled with her favorite bath salts that made her skin smooth and supple.

"Aw, this is nice." Sharon sighed. She tried desperately not to think about Bradley, but every time she closed her eyes, his face appeared in her mind. She heard her phone ringing in the bedroom and didn't want to get up from the tub, but the persistent ringing disturbed her peace. She rose from her bath and as soon as she put her feet onto the plush turquoise rug, she heard her doorbell ringing.

"Who in the world is that?" she asked. There was no time for her to get dressed. Sharon grabbed a towel and walked to the front door to see who was there. There stood the man in her mind.

"Oh no, it's Bradley!" She couldn't move fast enough away from the door.

"I can see you, Sharon. Please open the door. I really need to talk to you, baby. Please?"

She yelled through the door. "I have nothing to say to you. You lied to me, and I don't want to see you again." She knew that wasn't completely true. Feelings of hurt and shame arose within her.

"Sharon, I'm not leaving here until you talk to me. I'll camp out here all night if I have to."

She knew there was no turning back now; she had no choice but to open the door. Forgetting that she had her towel wrapped around her, she opened the door angrily.

Bradley stepped inside before she could change her mind. He knew this wouldn't be an easy conversation. He wanted the chance to explain to her. The thought of losing her over the illusion Catherine built wasn't an option. Immediately, he looked at her wet skin, and it was hard to take his eyes off her.

"What do you have to say to me? I think the show I got of you and your girlfriend said enough last night. Or shall I say, *fiancée*."

Bradley reared back. "She's not my fiancée—"

Sharon interrupted him. "We haven't known each other long, but I'd begun to let you into my life. How could you hurt me like this?"

"Please, let me explain." Bradley pleaded with his hands up and took a deep breath to slow his heart and his words. He needed to spell this out as calmly and clearly as possible. "I was going to tell you when I talked to you at the ranch. Between meeting you, my grandfather's passing, the drama with my brothers, and dealing with the estate, my life has been a whirlwind. The best thing about the last week has been you. Believe that. I wouldn't knowingly mess with that.

"All this with Catherine took me by surprise, and you left before I could tell you. I didn't even know she was in town. She and I dated years ago. I thought we were pretty serious. Obviously more than her." He looked over her shoulder, his eyes glazing over in thought.

"I played football in college. I was at an away game that ended early due to a thunderstorm. I came back to the apartment and found her and my roommate in bed together. She tried to tell me that it didn't mean anything and that was the first time it had happened, but I later found out that she would be there every time I wasn't in the apartment.

"To top it all off, she told my younger brother yesterday, the day of my grandfather's funeral, that her son is mine. I found that tidbit out this morning when he shuffled into the kitchen."

"Is he?"

"No."

"Are you sure?"

"Yes."

"Have you seen her since?" Sharon asked, watching him closely.

"She has tried to approach me through mutual friends in the past, but I told them I didn't want to talk to her. We aren't together, nor have we been for a long time."

"I think you can understand that this makes me want to put on the brakes between us. I'm thinking that I'm not asking you the right questions. I think there were ample opportunities for you and me to get to a discussion that may have led to her. At lunch, before the first time we kissed, before the first time you touched me and made me feel something for you... I don't like being caught off guard and being made to look like a fool. I've been through that before, and I won't do it again. I'll sooner say goodbye to you right now." She noticed Bradley had moved closer, and her heart softened a little at seeing the dark circles under his eyes. She remembered what Kera had said about him being concerned.

Bradley moved closer. The pleasure shown on his face at her lack of retreat. "I apologize, baby. I never meant to hurt you. I'll never intentionally make you feel like you're not wanted. Please let me make it up to you." Bradley pulled her into an embrace and passionately kissed her.

Her head swam, and she pried her mouth from his. "Wait. We need to talk. To get things clear."

"I feel things for you, Sharon, that I haven't felt for any other woman. I want to see where it goes. You've been my bright spot. I know you've felt it too because when I touch you, you burst into flames. I want to burn up with you," he said, dipping his head down to nuzzle at her neck where it met her shoulder and kissed his way back to her lips.

She was a goner and just like he'd stated, she caught fire. She tried with every molecule in her body to pull away, but his hold on her was stronger than she could fight. He cupped her bottom and caressed her lower back. He lifted her, carried her into the bedroom, and laid her on the king-sized bed. While he was still kissing her, he slowly removed the towel from around her body and eased himself on top of her.

"I want to make love to you. You're my heartbeat. When you exhale, I inhale everything about you, and this is how I breathe. I need you, baby. I want you to be my wife and bear my children. I can't fight these feelings I'm feeling. I'm in love with you, Sharon. I got to have you," he whispered in her ear.

Sharon was completely wrapped up in the emotion that her vulnerability took over. She gave in to the passionate touches he gave her. Her body became limp as he kissed her mouth and then to her neck. His hands caressed her breast, which sent blood rushing down her spine, around her waist, and into her innermost parts. The heat from their bodies engulfed the room.

She couldn't help but give in to the feelings and emotions surrounding his touch. She pulled up his shirt to reveal the toned muscles of his abdomen and then gently slid his shirt up over his head. She opened her eyes, which met his, and they both knew they were ready. Removing her lips from his sultry kiss, she kissed along his chest, sending the message to him that she was ready to share in the lovemaking they were about to engage in.

He made her body move as if they were in a yoga class. The way he positioned her relaxed every bone in her body. Inch by inch, he claimed her with his kisses and touch. The smell of the jasmine, with a hint of vanilla bubble bath she was in minutes before, seeped through her skin and made him aroused in a way he never experienced.

The firmness of his hands on her body drove her passionately insane. He ran his hands through her hair to release the pin that held it up in a bun while he continued kissing her. He slid his hand up her thigh and found her moist and inviting. He could tell by the way she felt and the way she moved, she wanted to make love just as much as he did. He touched a part of her soul that no man had ever done. Although she was there with him physically, her mind was somewhere else. Bradley wanted to make sure he was all she wanted and did whatever it took to have her think of only him. He pleasured every part of her body from her head down to her toes.

The moans and groans she made were those only he could make her have. He wanted to make sure she knew the love he felt was pure and unrelenting. He drew in a deep breath and released it as he slowly made her his. He carefully and thoroughly made love to her without hesitation, holding nothing back. They consummated their love throughout the night and fell into a deep sleep wrapped in each other's arms with total satisfaction.

The next morning, Sharon woke up early. She still felt the love she and Bradley had made the night before. She sat in the lounge chair in the corner of her bedroom, watching him as he slept.

Did we make the right decision to consummate our relationship?

Sharon had made a promise to herself—she would wait until after she was married before giving her body to a man again, but after last night, she was convinced that Bradley was the one she wanted to make love to for the rest of their lives. Their lovemaking was the best she ever felt. It made her feel things she'd been keeping inside for a long time, and it scared her. Mixed emotions came over her. She only knew that last night was amazing, and happiness consumed her. She knew that her feelings for Bradley were strong, but was it enough to build on?

Just then, he turned over. Looking around the room, he locked eyes with her. "Come back to bed, sweetheart," he said.

She was confused and didn't know what she wanted to do. Her eyes grew damp. Although it was slightly lit in the room, he saw the silhouette of her body. The sounds of a sniffle took him by surprise.

"What's wrong, honey?"

She held her head down to cry. Bradley saw that she was troubled by something. He put on his shorts that laid on the floor beside the bed. He walked over and kneeled down beside her. Gently rubbing her hands, he said, "Talk to me."

She continued to cry and tried not to look at him. "Last night didn't change anything, Bradley. It only complicated the situation."

"What are you talking about? It was a very special moment for us. I meant every word I said to you. Every action I did was because I love you."

"That's just it. I'm not sure if my love is enough for you."

"So, you're giving up on us? Last night, we made magic. I believe it was meant for us to be together. I don't want you to go, Sharon. Please, stay here with me and give us a chance. I promise I'll make you happier than you could ever imagine. I can't express how sorry I am for what happened, but it was never my intention to hurt you. You have to believe me... you have to believe in us."

"I think it's better that we get some distance for a while. I've been given an opportunity for us to expand our business in Paris. I've decided to take them up on the offer, so I'm leaving after the wedding. I'm not sure when I'll be back. As much as I don't want to go, I feel

I have to... for my sanity. I have to give them an answer. I need time for myself. The way you made love to me makes it that much more difficult."

"If it's that hard, then make it easy and stay with me." He leaned over and kissed her passionately, hoping this would help change her mind.

"I'm sorry, Bradley, but I have to figure out what *I* want, and I can't do it if I'm around you, knowing how I feel about you. To have you kiss me, touch me, and make love to me the way you did last night would be hard. It's too much, too soon, for me right now. Please don't make this any more complicated than it already is. Please."

He placed his arms around her and held her with his eyes burning. "I want you to know that I'm a man who won't give up on you... or us. Sharon, you're all I want, and I won't stop until I have you completely. You're my continual heartbeat. But I'll respect your wishes."

They embraced a little while longer, as if it would be the last time they would see each other. Watching him get dressed was an agonizing moment for her. She was so distraught that every piece of clothing he put on tore at her heart. Thoughts about whether she made the right decision to end the relationship with the man she loved tortured her. After he got dressed, she walked him to the door, and they said their goodbyes, both with tears in their eyes. He then got in his car, drove away. Watching his taillights fade into the distance became a moment in time she would never forget.

Chapter Nineteen

THE NEXT WEEK AND a half moved quickly with Kera's last few preparations causing her to be out of the office. Sharon not only took up the slack, she prepared for her trip to Paris. Her busy schedule more than her actual decision slowed things down with Bradley. She wouldn't say she was avoiding him. She just wasn't as available to see him, but they talked every night, giving her the sense of security she had needed.

The day had finally arrived for her best friend's wedding. As Sharon prepared to head out to the church for the ceremony, she looked at her phone and found a message from Bradley. stating how much he loved her, and how he hoped she knew that. A slight smile curled up from the corner of her mouth. She knew today would be a happy but difficult day for her. The man she had grown to love would be standing at the altar to witness their lifelong friends become one.

Lord, help me get through this day without breaking down.

She gathered everything she needed and headed out the door. On the drive to the church, Patsi called on the car phone. Sharon answered. She knew better than to *not* answer.

"Hello, Aunt Patsi."

"Hello. I just wanted to make sure you were okay and to see if you needed anything."

"I'm okay. I appreciate you checking up on me."

"I want you to remember that you're not only beautiful but successful. More importantly, you're a woman. It's okay to be vulnerable and feel hurt. That's what makes us distinctive from men. We know how to allow ourselves to feel and admit our weaknesses."

"Thank you for that. Thank you for the encouragement. I consider you a friend."

"Now don't go telling anyone that Aunt Patsi has a heart." She laughed.

"I won't tell anyone. It will be our little secret. Would you like me to pick you up? I could use the company."

"That would be lovely. I'm already ready to go."

"I'll see you in a few minutes," said Sharon.

***

Kera was a nervous wreck. "Where are my earrings? I can't find my favorite eyeshadow. I can't find anything!" she exclaimed.

"Calm down, honey," said Sara. "It's all right."

"Mom, what if I'm making a mistake? What if I don't make him happy? I…"

"Listen to me, baby girl. Take a deep breath and relax. You're going to make a beautiful bride and a beautiful wife. If he didn't think so, he wouldn't have asked you to marry him. When I met your father, I knew immediately that he would be my husband."

"How?" asked Kera.

"It was an indescribable inclination deep down inside me that told me he was the one. Yes, he made me feel safe and comfortable around him. His family was welcoming to me. He treated me with the utmost respect, but there was that assurance inside that let me know I was his rib carefully crafted just for him and only him. So, you see that's who you are to Gregg."

"Thanks, Mom," said Kera. "I'm so glad you're here."

"You're welcome, honey. Are you feeling better now?"

"Yes," Kera said even as another sob shook her.

Aunt Patsi and Sharon walked in to find the two of them embraced. Both were crying tears of joy.

"Oh no, is she sick?" cried Aunt Patsi.

"No," said Sara. "She's all right. Just wedding jitters."

"Oh, I thought maybe she was pregnant," said Patsi. All eyes turned to pierce her. "What? That's usually what happens at weddings. Somebody ends up pregnant." Patsi laughed aloud.

"Pregnant? Are you serious?" asked Kera.

"Just kidding, my niece. For goodness sake, it's just a little humor. Lighten up!"

"Don't pay her any attention, Kera," said Sharon. "You look amazing! I'm so excited for you."

"Thanks. Now please help me finish getting dressed."

"We're going out to make sure everything is all set up and that your father isn't still moping around," Sara said.

Sharon helped Kera with the buttons on her dress. Kera took her by the hand. "Are you all right, sis?"

"Yes. Why?"

"Have you spoken to him?" Kera asked.

"Yes, we spoke a few days ago, and we've spoken every day since."

"And how are things going?"

"Today is your day. We won't talk about my problems." Sharon picked up the makeup brush, swiping it across the palette of neutral eyeshadow colors. She turned to put it on Kera's face, trying to avoid the conversation.

"Don't do that, Sharon. You know I care about you. Gregg and I both want to see you happy. It doesn't matter what I have going on; you know I'll always make time for you. You're my best friend and sister. I want to know what happened."

"Okay. I told him I had a hard time with him keeping his interactions with Catherine a secret from me. He said she came to tell him her child is his, but he says it isn't. He doesn't want to end our relationship and honestly, I don't want to either. He has been very persistent in his pursual. He calls me a few times a day, and we're getting to know each other. I haven't trusted myself to be alone with him again since that day. I know he wants me to stay, but I'm so afraid of losing myself in him after..." She let the sentence trail off.

"All kind of thoughts roamed through my head on the way here. I was unfairly comparing him to my past relationship, and I realized he isn't like Mark. I believe that he does love me, but I can't say that I'm comfortable making that decision right now."

"I'm glad you haven't fully cut him off, but I do think you should be more open without waiting for the other shoe to fall. And you should look him in the eye the next time you two talk. You're stronger than you think. At least give him a chance to get this matter with Catherine cleared up so you can feel more confident in your relationship with him. You don't want to have this hanging over your head, thinking about the what ifs. Don't do that to yourself," said Kera.

"I know you're right. I'll give him a chance. I'll talk to him again after the wedding, but right now, we have a lot of work to do to get you ready." Kera jumped up with joy.

"That's the Sharon I know. Get your man, honey! You see you've found your Boaz." They both burst out into laughter.

***

The church was decorated in gray and mahogany colors. Tulips aligned the pulpit with red and white roses on every pew. The atmosphere was full of love. The seating area was filled to capacity. Family, friends, colleagues, and clients of Sharon and Kera's came to share in the joining of Kera and Gregg. One could feel genuine happiness from each and every guest.

As Kera and Gregg said their vows to each other, Sharon couldn't help but notice Bradley's eyes on her. She tried desperately not to look at him, but she found her attention straying to him time and time again. She just had to get through this wedding with the same determination she had the week. It would be harder with him so close but if she was going to make a clear-headed decision about them, she couldn't give in to the promise of pleasure in his eyes.

At the reception, Sharon and Bradley had to give the maid of honor and best man speech. Side by side, they stood facing the bride and groom, while everyone watched them give their heartfelt blessings to the married couple. Bradley went first.

"Greg. You and I have been friends for a long time and though when we were kids, we acted like kids, I've seen you grow into the man you are today. I couldn't be more pleased to see that you've made a choice any man would be proud of in Kera. The two of you were cut from the same star, and I can't wait to see what you do together." He paused and looked over at Sharon.

"I look forward to following in your footsteps soon, my brother," Bradley continued into the mic, never taking his eyes off of Sharon.

Sharon knew her eyes had gone wide at his innuendo. The murmurs from the attendees punctuated his meaning, and she couldn't help but feel embarrassed. He was all but proclaiming his intentions towards her in front of all of their friends and family. He wasn't playing fair but for obvious reasons, she couldn't be upset. He had made it plain to her that he wanted them to be together. She just needed a little more time.

Sharon cleared her throat and tore her gaze from Bradley's. "Kera and Gregg, I couldn't be happier to know that you have one another and are secure in that love. I've seen the way you two handle situations. You do it together with open communication, and I believe that will get you farther than anything. Enjoy each other. Enjoy your life together, and as the pastor said, 'We praise God for blessing this union.'" She raised her glass and took a sip with everyone before taking Bradley's outstretched hand and allowing him to guide her back to her seat at Kera's right before returning to his seat at Gregg's left. She was both a little relieved and disappointed at his distance. She chuckled to herself. She was all confused, and it was no one's fault but hers. She distracted herself by diverting all of her attention to the next few toasts and goings on at the reception.

Eventually, it was time for the bride and groom's first dance. Kera had on a Vera Wang white strapless wedding dress, with pearls layered on the front and pearls for buttons along the back. It was fitted in the waist and flared out like a Cinderella ballgown on the bottom. Her makeup was flawless. It had only taken two tries after by the makeup artist after she and Aunt Patsi had arrived to find Kera and her mom balling. She wore natural tones that made her skin glow like the sun. The stylist twisted her hair into a loose side French bun, with some pieces trailing down the side of her face. The bun was adorned with pearl hair accessories.

Anyone with eyes could see that Gregg stood in awe of his bride. It was obvious that he treasured her and was a perfect match for her in his tuxedo. He wore a white Egara slim-fit shawl lapel dinner jacket, with Calvin Klein black slacks and black Cole Haan Oxfords with a tap toe.

As they danced and stared into each other's eyes, they were the picture of love and adoration. They were in a world all on their own.

The wedding party soon joined them on the dance floor. The song "Ready or Not" started played, as Bradley took Sharon in his arms and led her effortlessly on the dance floor. Sharon gave in to the moment and allowed her head to rest on his chest. No words had to be spoken. She just followed him and concentrated on trying to hear his heartbeat over the music. His cologne was intoxicating, wrapping any senses that weren't already captured by his touch up in a hazy cocoon. Her body swayed with his, and it was only natural to feel his lips at her temple from time to time.

"I want to hold you forever. It's hard for me to be this close to you and not want to protect, cherish, and throw you over my shoulder so I can take you somewhere quiet."

She couldn't help the laugh that bubbled from her lips. He was incorrigible but honest. If she were truthful, she felt much the same as he did. She bit her lip slightly. With the song playing in the background and the feel of each movement in his hands as he massaged her back, it was hard not looking up at him and telling him to do just that.

"I need to tell you something. It's very important," she said. She was ready to tell Bradley that she wanted him, and she would be willing to let her guard down. He had been patient and open, giving her the time and confidence she needed in them to go to Paris without wondering if he remained faithful.

Bradley looked down at her and was about to kiss her when he did a doubletake at something, and his whole body went stiff.

Sharon felt his hands slipping away. She followed his eyes across the room, and there stood the woman she had only recently reconciled to the farthest corners of her mind.

As soon as the song was over, Bradley guided Sharon from the dance floor off to the side where they could be alone, but Catherine stayed on their heels.

They walked out a side door that led to another parking area. Suddenly, Bradley took Sharon into his arms as if to protect her from Catherine, who stood by watching.

He leaned back far enough to hold Sharon's gaze as he whispered desperately, "I don't know why she's here. I told you everything I know, so please, please..."

Catherine's impatient tone interrupted his plea. "Bradley, we need to talk."

He turned to her, keeping Sharon at his side but angled slightly behind him in a stance of protection.

"Why are you here?"

"I was invited by the bride," said Catherine. She walked slowly towards them. "I'm glad I came."

Kera may have initially invited the woman to her wedding, but Sharon was pretty sure that invite had been revoked since the drama at the funeral. Bradley wasn't fooled

"I don't have time for this," said Bradley. "You need to leave." His eyebrows grew closer together, and he felt the vein in the middle of his forehead pulse.

"Oh, so you want me to leave so you can run off with your fairy tale ending. I don't think so. Sharon, did he tell you that we made love at his grandfather's ranch two weeks ago? That he told me he loved me and wanted to be with me?"

"What is she talking about, Bradley?" Sharon asked.

The hurt in her eyes made Bradley even more furious. He had worked so hard to remove that wounded look. They were still early days, but he already knew that his end game was a day like this for them with her walking down the aisle, her having his children, and eventually, the two of them watching their grandchildren grow up.

"I don't know what her deluded mind is telling her, baby, but that's not true. I never slept with her, and I sure as hell didn't tell her that I loved her." He hated the desperation in his voice, but he was afraid.

"Deluded, am I? I wasn't deluded when we were making our son. You don't know how much you hurt me. How much I waited to have you come back to me and our family. How can you choose this woman over our family? You won't be able to avoid your responsibilities once my lawyers deal with you."

"Wow! You're crazier than I thought. Catherine, you need help, and that's something I can't give you. There's no us, and we'll never be to-gether. Get that through your head. Tell that to the other men you've been with. We've been over for a long time because you couldn't keep your legs closed," Bradley said.

"Enough," said Sharon. "You two need to work this out. I can't deal with it." She turned to walk away. Bradley grabbed her arm to keep her from leaving.

"No, baby. There's nothing I need to work out with this woman. She just needs to get a grip on reality. We won't let her come between what we have. She's just trying to make problems. She's jealous and wants what she can't have." He took Sharon by her hand and tried to walk away from Catherine.

"No, Bradley. You stay and work this out," said Sharon. She looked deep into his eyes, trying to convey her determination to avoid these scenes, these types of women, this drama in her life. She continued on a whisper, "Get your house in order. " When he began to shake his head, she placed a palm on his cheek to stop him, then kissed him softly before turning to Catherine.

"I know women like you. You're beautiful, successful, and very talented at manipulating men to get what you want to get to the top. You're a bitter, sad woman, and women like you soon get what they deserve. I'm not angry with you; I feel sad for you." Shaking her head in disbelief, Sharon walked back into the church. She knew then that she had to decide to do what was best for her. She couldn't tell Bradley how she truly felt. She needed some time to focus on herself. The last thing she needed or wanted in her life was drama and definitely not having to deal with a contentious woman.

"Sharon, please wait... don't go," Bradley begged, as he walked after her. He wanted to convince her to stay with him, but she kept walking away. Then Catherine pulled him back.

"Let her go! She'll never make you as happy as I can. I'm the only woman who knows what you want and what you need," cried Catherine. She slid her hand across his chest affectionately.

"Please get away from me!" he yelled in irritation. This drew the attention of some of the guests that were close by, especially Aunt Patsi.

"I don't want to talk to you, Catherine. Please leave. I don't want you! When will you understand that? You messed that up a long time ago. You've caused enough problems already. I'm done with you and all of this," said Bradley.

"Problems?" she asked. "You don't know the meaning of the word problems. If you don't talk to me, you'll wish that you had. I didn't make our son on my own, and I surely won't raise him on my own either. So, you better want to talk to me. I'm not leaving here until you do."

"Oh, you're threatening me now? Is that it? Well, guess what? You can bring your little lawyers and whoever else you want. I'm leaving. You can talk to yourself. Trying to threaten me, you've definitely lost your mind. Get over yourself, lady, and if it's money you're trying to get, it isn't happening." Bradley started walking away, all the while furious, and immediately turned to face her with nothing but contempt in his heart for her.

"You come here almost four years later to tell me that I have a kid with you. If you were pregnant by me, you should have said something then. You don't wait this long to tell a man he's a father. Let's allow the court to decide whether or not the child is mine. If he is, I'll make sure he's taken care of, but there will never be anything between us. Never! Do you hear me?"

Catherine shrank back a little. He saw the persistent gleam in her eyes. She wouldn't give up so easily. "If that's what you want, then that's what we'll do. You'll be sorry."

"What's going on out here?" asked Aunt Patsi. "Everyone at the reception can hear all the fuss."

"There's nothing for you to be concerned about. Go back inside! Besides, you need to mind your business and stay out of mine. This doesn't need a geriatric intervention!" yelled Catherine.

"Little girl, I've warned you before not to mess with grown folk. Now, this is a wedding. We don't allow any animals in the vicinity. So, take your paws and put them to use by walking out of here before I send you out on what little behind you have," said Patsi.

"Who do you think you're talking to? Would you please rejoin your knitting class with your old behind. You clearly don't know who you're messing with."

"I don't care if you were the Queen of Africa. If you don't get away from here, I'll show you what this fine old woman will do to you."

"You don't have to worry about me, I know what I came here for, and I'm not leaving here without him," said Catherine.

"You're so delusional. It's clear the man doesn't want you. Accept that and move on with your miserable life. He's too much of a gentleman to put his hands on a woman or disrespect her. I, on the other hand, I'll lay hands on you." She took off her heels and asked Clint, who had come out to see what the commotion was, to hold them for her. She was in the middle of removing her earrings when Clint picked her up and pulled her back towards the party.

"What are you doing?" asked Clint, gently letting her down when they were a few yards away.

"I'm about to whip her tail. She doesn't know me. She came here trying to mess with my nieces. I'll handle that little tramp." Patsi's breathing grew heavier and heavier as she tried to push her way around Clint.

"No, ma'am! You're too much of a lady for that. May I add, a sexy lady," said Clint.

Patsi smoothed back her hair, pulled down her dress, and straightened it from where he picked her up and smiled at the young man. She took in a few deep breaths, noticing that even more people had come out to see what all of the yelling was about. She wouldn't be the one making the biggest scene at her niece's wedding. She looked up at the man wo had saved her from herself.

"Boy, you're pretty strong; don't think I don't know what you're trying to do. I'll let you have this moment, with your cute self."

"I'm stronger than you think," Clint admitted.

"Well, well now, we'll just have to see about that." Patsi chuckled low, and looking back, she had distracted Catherine just long enough for Bradley to make his escape. Well, she had to give Clint two points for his interruption.

"I look forward to showing you what I can do someday." He kissed her hand and escorted her back to the reception area.

Kera and Gregg were on the dance floor when Sharon walked up to them. Greg was startled by the difference in her demeanor. Just a few minutes before, she was following Bradley off the dance floor with stars in her eyes.

"I have to go. I'm sorry it's so abrupt, but Bradley should be able to explain everything." She reached over and kissed Kera on the cheek and gave him a quick hug.

"I'm gonna go ahead and leave tonight so don't be worried if I don't pick up my phone for a few hours. Okay? I love you, and I'm so happy for you too. I'll call you, Kera, as soon as I land at Heathrow."

Gregg reached out, trying to stall her departure, but Sharon was gone as quickly as she appeared. He looked down at his new bride who looked just as baffled as he felt.

He kissed his wife. "I'm going to look for Bradley. You see if you can't stop Sharon."

Kera nodded and moved swiftly in the direction Sharon had left.

Gregg noticed that Bradley was walking around the church and caught him as he went by. "What's up, man?"

"Have you seen Sharon?"

"Yeah, she just told us that she was leaving to get ready for her flight," said Gregg.

"Her flight? It isn't scheduled until tomorrow afternoon, right?"

"Well, she decided to take an early one. That's why she left."

"What? I have to catch her. I can't let her go." Bradley glanced around.

"I couldn't reach her before she left. What's going on?" asked Kera, stepping up to them. "Everyone was talking about some commotion between you, some unknown woman, Sharon, and Aunt Patsi. What did you do?"

"I'll tell you later," said Bradley. "Enjoy your honeymoon. I love you both." He kissed Kera, congratulated them, and ran towards the parking lot.

"Bradley!" Gregg yelled. It was too late. He wouldn't turn back now to talk. He was on a mission to get the love of his life back, and that was more important to him than anything in the world.

Chapter Twenty

Bradley's car left the church parking lot with tremendous speed, his mind racing a mile a minute. He drove to Sharon's house, hoping to catch her there before heading to the airport. As he turned into her driveway, he received a text message from Gregg, informing him that Sharon was at the airport, and her flight was scheduled to leave at six fifteen p.m. Bradley looked at his watch. It was now five thirty p.m. Time was of the essence. He knew that if he didn't get there in time, he wouldn't see the woman he loved again.

Bradley drove as fast as he could to Columbia Metropolitan Airport. He watched as plane after plane exited the runway, hoping for a miracle, and anticipating that he could stop her from leaving. Bradley parked his car, ran up the sidewalk to the entrance, and frantically walked up to an attendant to ask if the flight to Paris had left yet. He took a deep breath, praying on the inside as the attendant looked up the information for the flight.

Bradley shook uncontrollably. His nerves had taken over completely. Thoughts raced through his mind, as he waited for the news. Wringing his hands together, Bradley bit his bottom lip and shifted his weight from one leg to the other. "Oh Lord, please don't let me be too late," he pleaded.

"I'm sorry, sir. That flight just left the runway," the attendant informed him. "The next flight to Paris is tomorrow at 11:25 a.m. with two layovers in Charlotte and New York. Would you like to book that flight?"

Bradley looked at the attendant downheartedly and replied, "No, that won't be necessary. Thank you and have a good evening." Bradley took a slow stroll back to his car. He sat there, thinking of how he should have tried harder to stop Sharon from leaving the church. Maybe she wouldn't have left so soon. His heart throbbed hard against his chest, as if a heart attack was about to take over his body. The phone rang, and Bradley took it out of his pocket in hopes it was Sharon. He was disappointed to see his brother Charles' name on the display.

"Hello, Charles."

"Where are you, man? I've been calling all over for you. We need to talk. I need you to come back to the house as quickly as you can," Charles pleaded.

"What's going on? Is it Ken? Are you guys all right?"

"Yes, we're fine. When can you get to the ranch? I have some information I need to share with you. Can you meet me in say an hour?"

"What information are you talking about?"

"I can't tell you over the phone," said Charles. "Just know that it is vitally important, all right?"

"Okay, I'm coming. I'm on my way there now." It seemed he would have to let Sharon go for the moment and try to do what she'd requested. He needed to clean house. Hopefully, what Charles needed to talk to him about would add to the mess he was already dealing with.

When Bradley arrived at the ranch, he saw an unfamiliar car with an Illinois license plate in the driveway. Ken, who was smoking a cigarette on the front porch, greeted him as he walked up the steps. Ken was known for not being able to hide his facial expressions, and today was no different. Bradley could tell that whatever his brothers needed to discuss with him was serious.

"Come on, brother. They're waiting for you in the living room," said Ken. Bradley was nervous and excited at the same time. He wondered what his brothers had up their sleeves. Ken and Charles were known for playing practical jokes on him in the past, and he wasn't in the mood for their games today.

Bradley tugged on his brother's arm and asked, "Who's here? I've never seen that car."

"Come in. You'll see. Don't worry brother; everything's going to be fine." Ken smiled.

"Hey Bradley, please sit down. This is my good friend Tom Carter." Charles said, gesturing to a man about six foot with a barrel chest. His whiskey-colored eyes were friendly in his otherwise serious face, which consisted of a high forehead, wide nose, and high cheekbones. He reminded Bradly of a Sioux brave but with paperback-brown skin. "He's one of the best private investigators I know."

Bradley reached out to shake the man's hand, still confused as to why the man was in his house.

"It's nice to meet you. Does anybody want to tell me what's going on?"

"I asked Tom to do some investigating on your friend Catherine."

"You did what? Without even asking me?"

"I'm sorry, but I couldn't sit around and watch you go through so much pain and agony surrounding this woman," Charles responded.

"So, you involve a stranger in my life. What were you thinking?"

"Calm down and listen to what he has to say," said Ken.

"You were in on this too, little brother?" Bradley placed his hand on his chest.

"Hey, we were both worried about you. You've taken care of me all my life; I just wanted to return the favor. I know how much Sharon means to you. We both do. We see the look in your eyes when you're together," said Ken.

"Remember we're DuPont men. No one is going to try to take advantage of us. Please hear what he has to say," said Charles.

"Okay, let's hear it." Bradley leaned back onto the chair and crossed his legs.

Tom took out a small, worn pocket notebook. Flipping it open, he recited his findings, "I investigated one Catherine Morris, formally residing at a home on Westminster Abbey Drive in Sacramento, California, by way of Chicago, Illinois for three years beginning three years ago. She became romantically involved with Mr. Pall Stevenson, one of the directors at the accounting firm where she was employed in Sacramento before being relocated to Chicago. He filed a complaint against her for harassment and stalking him and his family. She claimed that she became pregnant by Mr. Stevenson after two years and was provided a lump sum of money to help her relocate from Illinois. An ongoing restraining order is in place against her. Once Mr. Stevenson learned through a DNA test that he wasn't the father, he cried foul and began legal proceedings against her to retrieve the money."

"Wait a minute! So, what does this mean?" Bradley jumped up from the chair and stood in the middle of the living room, pounding his fist in rage. "Are you telling me that because her cash cow dried up, she's trying to pin me as her child's father? I knew she was foul, but I didn't expect her to be so obvious in her plight. How do we prove I'm not the father?"

"How do you know you're not the father?" asked Charles.

"What do you mean how do I know? What kind of question is that?" asked Bradley. "I stopped being physical with Catherine around the beginning of February, more than three years ago. Tell me when the baby was born?"

"The birth certificate shows she gave birth in October, a little over three years ago," said Tom.

"So, you're saying there's a possibility that the child is mine?" Bradley shook his head in disbelief. "She tried to ruin my life with her lies. How evil can a person be? I don't think I'm the father of her son. I want to take a paternity test as soon as possible. I want everyone to know the truth."

Bradley sat on the sofa, next to the fireplace where his grandfather used to sit when he needed to decide something. He looked around, pondering in his head the possibilities of having a son with a woman he couldn't stand, and how it could affect his chances of ever being happy with Sharon. Just then, Gregg called to check on him. He told Gregg all about the situation with Catherine and how he feared he could lose Sharon.

"Keep your head up and don't lose hope. Sharon is a loving and forgiving woman. When all else seems hopeless, believe in the love you two have developed for each other. To be honest with you, I never trusted Catherine when you two were dating. She was too clingy. Well,

I must go. I'll call you once we return from Cabo San Lucas in a few days," said Gregg.

"All right, man! Have a wonderful honeymoon," said Bradley.

While Charles made calls to see if he could get his brother a paternity test as soon as possible, Bradley paced the floor. Ken walked over to him and placed his hand on his shoulder.

"It's going to be all right, big brother. We're here for you; I hope you know that."

"I know, and I'm grateful. I'm so torn and hurt at the same time. Gramps isn't settled in the grave yet, and I get hit with this. Not to mention, I could lose the only woman who ever made me feel alive and wanted as a man. Ken, I must make things right between me and Sharon."

Ken looked at him with compassion, but he couldn't help but chuckle at what his brother said. Bradley's face instantly took on a look of instant fury.

"What's so funny?"

"Oh, forgive me. I'm not laughing at you. I just realized that after all these years, my brother the businessman, who said he would never fall in love, has gone against his own vow. You've been bitten by the love bug, and it just makes me so happy to finally see the joy in you. Gramps said it would happen soon. I guess the old man was right."

Bradley couldn't help but smile in agreement, "Yes, he was."

Charles finally received a call from a facility that could do the testing for them. "Tomorrow morning? That sounds perfect. We'll be there. Thank you so much for getting back to me so soon. Have a good day."

Bradley and Ken stood in the hall when they heard part of the conversation their brother had on the phone. "Was that about the paternity test?" asked Bradley.

"Yes, I made you an appointment for tomorrow morning at 8 o'clock. Will that work for you?"

"Yes, that's perfect. The sooner I can get it done, the sooner I can move on with my life."

"You would have to wait about two to three weeks and maybe even longer before the results can be mailed to you."

"Two to three weeks or longer? I'm not sure I can wait that long. The suspense is killing me now. By then, it may be too late. Sharon has already left for Paris."

"It is possible to have the results back within three to five business days for a routine test. It depends on whether she cooperates and whether she takes the child to be tested. If she's telling the truth, then you should have the results back in that timeframe. If she isn't, I'm afraid you could be waiting a while, and I would have to get a court order in place," said Charles.

Bradley sank into the chair, with his head in his hands. Everyone in the room felt the pain rolling off him in waves. The three watched as the room grew heavy with emotion and silence.

"Thanks, everyone, for your help," said Bradley before he got up and walked to his room.

Chapter Twenty-One

Sharon arrived in Paris and took a taxi to the Hotel Ritz, where she would be staying for the duration of her trip. She was overtaken by the lights and atmosphere of the city, and it gave her such peace. Still, she couldn't escape the memories and feelings of what she had left behind in the States. She loved Bradley so much, but she couldn't bear the thought of losing him to another woman. Especially a woman who claimed to have given birth to his child.

After feeling the effects of the long flight, Sharon decided she would take a long, hot bath. Afterward, she settled down for a nap before going out for a bite to eat. Sharon wanted to see some of Paris as a tourist before work started. Her meeting with the investors wouldn't be until Wednesday, which would give her time to rest and get in some sightseeing.

Soaking while staring at the Eiffel Tower in the distance from her hotel bathroom window, she tried to make sense of the turn of events that had taken place in her and Bradley's lives. Thoughts of the many conversations they had, where she felt the connection was much deeper than the physical. He cared about her. He listened to her innermost thoughts and asked attentive questions, showing his interest and undivided attention. He made her feel special.

Their lovemaking had been mind altering, and she had been ready to surrender to him. She would have if it weren't for that woman who showed up. She hadn't wanted a relationship filled with shadows from their pasts hovering over them. She wanted to love Bradley in the light of the sun, free of the doubts in herself and in them.

And there it was, like lightning in a storm, allowing her to see in the darkest recesses of her mind. It wasn't about the messiness surrounding Bradley. It wasn't even about the lack of transparency in their relationship, though sorely needed to be addressed.

It was about the promise she made to herself after her relationship with Mark. It was about all of the conversations she had in the mirror with herself, the times she reminded herself how valuable she was, how God saw her, and the times she promised herself that she would put her relationship with God in front of men. It was about the times she told herself she would love herself more. More than her job or any man. This was about her and keeping her word to herself.

She would open up the new office and get back in touch with herself so that when or if she and Bradley got back together, she wouldn't only maintain her identity, she would do it the way God intended it. She had gotten lost in the pining for family. How could she ask for a Boaz if she wasn't willing to be a Ruth.

***

Patsi paced the floors worrying about Sharon and the way things ended at the reception. She had grown extremely fond of her. Painful memories of the child she had given up for adoption after the death of her first husband pierced her like a knife. At the time, she felt she wasn't ready to be a mother. She knew she wasn't emotionally stable enough to care for her. She imagined the kind of mother she would have been to a beautiful daughter such as Sharon.

I believe I would have been a wonderful mother.

Patsi decided to give Sharon a call to make sure she was okay. Before dialing Sharon's number, she noticed that Clinton had texted her. It read, "Hi, beautiful. Just checking on you. I would love to take you to dinner." She paused for a minute and said to herself, "Yeah, right. I bet you would like to take me to dinner. Hey, but I still got it. I might have to school this young man on the difference between a woman and a girl." She was laughing so much, she almost forgot to call Sharon.

Sharon had just stepped out of the huge tub and was about to get into bed when she saw her phone light up. She was a little hesitant about looking to see who it was. She feared it would be Bradley trying to reach her again. He had left her eight messages. His voice messages were full of how much he loved her and how he didn't want to lose her. She was about to turn her ringer off, but she realized it was Aunt Patsi.

"Hello, Aunt Patsi," she answered.

"Hey! Baby girl, I'm not going to keep you long. I just wanted to check on you and to see if you made it to Paris safely."

"Yes, ma'am. I'm all right. We had a small bit of turbulence coming over the ocean, but it smoothed out once we were about five hours out."

"I'm glad nothing happened. Are you sure you're okay? Aunt Patsi just got to make sure you're absolutely all right."

"I'm a little jetlagged, but I'm good."

"Okay, I'm here if you need me. I hope you know that."

"Yes, I know, and Aunt Patsi, please don't tell you know who that we've spoken. I'm not ready to talk with him just yet."

"I understand. You just take all the time you need, and I'll check in on you tomorrow. Have a good night."

"Thanks! You do the same also. Good night!"

As soon as Sharon hung up the phone, Kera called her. She knew that if she didn't answer, Kera would keep calling until she picked up. She had kept her promise to call when she reached Heathrow and again when she reached her hotel, but she needed some time to think. Also, she didn't want to infringe on her friend's honeymoon and time with her new husband. She missed her girl. She missed talking to her, but she had to do some of this on her own.

"Hi, Kera. How's the honeymoon coming along? I know it's beautiful there. I'm loving Paris. It's an amazing place to be this time of year." Sharon was talking so much, she didn't give her friend enough time to say anything. Kera finally had to intercept the conversation.

"Sharon, I know you're talking a lot to keep me from asking about how you're doing, and that's okay. Firstly, let me start by saying that I'm sorry you're going through this. If you need me, I'll be here. All you have to do is say the word. Secondly, I want you to know that I'm very proud to have you as my sister. You're an amazing person and no matter what, you'll always be amazing to all of us."

Sharon found it hard to hold back her tears. One managed to escape from the corner of her eye. "Thank you, and you know the feeling is mutual. I don't want you worrying about me. I'll be all right. I'm in a new city, and the people seem to be very nice here. I'm seizing the moment to enjoy myself and focus on me, for a change."

"Okay, but don't have too much fun before I get there in three weeks. Oh, and by the way, I canceled our contract with Catherine. Even though the money would have been wonderful, I don't want to do business with conniving people."

"I'm sure that didn't go well with her," said Sharon.

"No, and she tried to say she would sue us for not completing the job. I told her nicely that she needed to make sure she read the fine print. Clearly, she didn't, because if she had, she wouldn't have taken that tone with me.

"She now understands that the contract is null and void if the client isn't in compliance with the terms of the contract. She lied to us about so many things, and you know I found out that the house wasn't hers. It was her boss'. The poor, unsuspecting man is out of the country for a few months. She wasn't even supposed to be in it. I found out she was having an affair with the man. Even if none of that were true, and the contract was harder to get out of, I couldn't, knowing I was doing business with someone who hurt my sister."

"That's not surprising. She's a piece of work. I can say that."

"You know I'm going to ask, so I'll come right out with it. Have you spoken with Bradley?"

"No. He's left me so many messages, I haven't had a chance to read them all. I just need some time to envelop myself in peace before talking to him," said Sharon.

"I know, my friend, and when you're ready, I'm sure you'll make the best decision for you. Just an FYI, Gregg said he spoke with Bradley last night, and he's not giving up on you."

"Well, it's not only his decision. Besides, he has work to do with keeping his past in the past," replied Sharon.

"That may be true, but I'm going to say this... Bradley is a persistent man. Don't be surprised if he's waiting at your house when you get back. You love him too. You know we love to be chased, especially by a man as fine as him," Kera said, laughing.

"Yes, we do. Fine or not, I just don't want to let that get in the way of what I need to do for me."

"You didn't ask my opinion, but I think you should make him wait for you to do what you need to do for you."

Sharon thought aloud and didn't think Kera had heard her when she said, "Girl, it's too late for that."

"What? You mean you and Bradley have been intimate, and you didn't tell me? I'm hurt."

"Don't be so dramatic, Kera, and yes, we made love a few weeks ago. It has complicated things between us, and that's why I had to leave. I can't bear the thought of losing him to Catherine and their son. It's too much for me. It seems I'm facing the same situation all over again."

"I hear your concerns, and I totally understand how you're feeling. I don't want you to give up without a fight. Don't coward down to your feelings without knowing the truth. Between you and me, Bradley is having a paternity test done soon."

"A paternity test?" asked Sharon. She didn't think it was even possible that Bradley was the father of Catherine's child.

"Yes. From what Gregg said, Bradley didn't even think it was a possibility until he met with a private investigator. I've already said too much, but I wanted you to know, so don't make any drastic decisions without knowing the results first. I believe what you and Bradley have is meant to be."

"Only God knows if that's true, Kera, and I pray that all works out for him. I want him to be happy. Well, you better get back to your husband. I'm about to take a nap before getting something to eat. I love you, girl, and tell Gregg hello," said Sharon.

"Okay, see you soon," said Kera.

Sharon thought about her conversation with Kera after she'd taken her bath. She'd had enough excitement within the past few hours and was too exhausted to think about anything else. She lay down on the bed with hopes of falling into a peaceful sleep. It would give her mind and heart a rest from everything.

Chapter Twenty-Two

Bradley was on edge, waiting to hear when he could take the paternity test. After five days of waiting, he was nearly climbing the walls. He'd hardly slept at all. He'd stayed up half the night, questioning whether he indeed was the father of Catherine's baby and hoping he could make this all go away. He wondered if Sharon missed him as much as he missed her, and if she would ever forgive him.

He was pulled out of his thoughts by Charles' phone ringing. "Hello?"

Bradley didn't move from his place on the couch with his head resting on the back, eyes closed. The sound of movement caused him to peer at Charles through one slitted eye. The intense look on Charles' face had him opening both eyes.

"Yes. Today at 11 a.m." Charles checked his watch. "Yes, that's perfect," said Charles. "We'll be there," Charles said before hanging up.

"What??" asked Bradley.

"Get dressed. We have an appointment with the testing center in an hour and a half. So, move quickly," said Charles. Ken, who had been lounging in one of the club chairs, was all smiles.

"It shouldn't take you too long to get dressed. I'm going to change too," Ken said before leaving the room.

Bradley spared Charles a look conveying his gratitude before running to his room to change out of his sweats.

As they got into the car, Ken could tell that his brother was a nervous wreck. None of the men said a word until they reached the clinic. Charles switched off the engine and took off his seatbelt to open the door. He then looked back at Bradley.

"Don't worry, brother; everything is going to be all right," said Charles.

"Yeah, man," said Ken. "We're here now. We'll take it one battle at a time."

"I appreciate all your help. You guys are the best brothers any man could ask for," said Bradley.

The three of them walked into the clinic. Once inside, Bradley signed in, and they all sat, waiting nervously for his name to be called. Then finally, the nurse came out and called his name to come back with her to be tested. Bradley got up, but he didn't look back at his brothers.

Charles and Ken looked at each other with concern. Ken leaned over to his brother and whispered, "I need a smoke break. Would you like to come and join me?"

"You know I don't smoke, man, but I'll come out with you. It shouldn't take that long for the test."

They both walked outside. Ken had his cigarettes in one hand and his lighter in the other. As he lifted the cigarette to his mouth, he stated, "I really hope this isn't his baby. He deserves to have a family with someone he loves. I know. This woman has some serious problems. If it's his child, he'll do the right thing and take care of his kid. She's going to make it hard for him."

"Yeah. We'll be here to support him if he needs us. Remember DuPonts are honorable men, no matter what the circumstance," replied Charles.

The two men continued standing outside as they waited on Bradley to finish up with the test. They were laughing and talking about a few past relationships that had scared them. This was how Bradley found them when he exited the building.

Charles glanced over and saw him coming out towards them. "You're all done?" he asked.

"Yes. Let's go!" Bradley exclaimed.

As they pulled out of the clinic's parking lot, heading into traffic, Ken asked, "So, did they mention when the results will be back?"

"The nurse said that the sooner Catherine comes in with the child, the sooner we can get the results. She also said it could take several weeks. If I know Catherine, she'll try to drag this out as long as she can. There's no way I'll let her sit down on this. The sooner this is done, the sooner I can resume my life. I'm going to call her to make sure she comes today so we can get this over with."

"No, Bradley! We have to do this the right way and the legal way. If not, you may never know the truth, and you could have this hanging over your head for a long time. If she doesn't come in within the next day or so, I can get the paperwork started to subpoena her to court. We have to make sure we do this by the books, so we don't have to worry about the repercussions later. Please, promise me that you won't approach her until we get to the bottom of this? Promise me!" Charles exclaimed.

"You know I don't like making promises I may not keep, but I'll try my best not to talk to her."

"If she contacts you for anything, we can also get a restraining order against her."

"You see what good it did the last guy? You've witnessed what kind of monster she is. There's no telling what lengths she'll go to make my life miserable. I just want her completely out of my life."

Jokingly, Ken said, "Yeah, she's a piece of work. Also, did you see that Aunt Patsi was about to tear her to pieces?"

"That would have been the thing to watch. That lady doesn't play any games. She looks as if she'll beat the skin off you if you cross her," said Charles.

"Yes, Aunt Patsi is something else. I like her though. She believes in standing up for the people she cares about for sure," said Bradley. They all laughed. For a moment, it seemed as if they didn't have a care in the world. Just three brothers enjoying a drive home and having a good time together; it felt like old times.

Then Bradley turned his head towards the window and stared as if someone was calling him that only he could see. He couldn't help but think of Sharon. He had flooded her voicemail and inbox with messages but to no avail. He had yet to receive a response from her. The more time they were away from each other, the more his hope faded

***

To pass the time until Charles could get the slow legal process moving to force Catherine to get her child tested, Bradley threw himself deep into his work. He worked extra late, making sure he didn't fall behind with his business work or on the ranch. It was calming to him to think about something other than his own problems. Not to mention take his mind off missing Sharon. It would be a long process trying to get her out of his system.

***

The courts finally caught up with Catherine to submit to taking the paternity test and thus started yet another wait for Bradley. Though Sharon had begun to respond to some of his text messages, she'd only called him once in the weeks since her departure. It had been sweet torture hearing her voice, but the time and distance had him on edge and more than a little desperate. He had asked her if he could come see her. She hadn't said yes or no. She simply asked if he had done what she'd asked him at the reception.

He hadn't handled it well. His frustration had gotten the better of him, and the phone call had ended much sooner than he was ready.

Doubt set in even more. It sounded simple. Deal with his past, but everything in this situation made it more complicated than he could control, and the more time passed, the more his mind told him that he may have lost Sharon for good, and he should try to get her out of his mind. He knew it would be hard to erase her from ever being a part of his life. He reflected on her smile, the way her lips moved when he kissed her, and the way her body felt when he touched her. No one could ever make him feel the way she did. The thought of not having her tour him up inside.

Gregg and Kera had returned from their honeymoon, and they looked so happy together. If love truly existed, the two of them were a positive reassurance.

Kera continued servicing the clients back in South Carolina, and business was still growing just as it was before. She missed having Sharon in the office with her and couldn't wait to join her in two days. Kera felt the two of them worked better together. For the past two years, they had prepared for the opportunity to expand in Paris. Now that it had happened, it all seemed so surreal. She couldn't wait to get to Paris to see what new and exciting creations Sharon had designed so far in the homes there.

It was time for Kera to leave the office to prepare for her trip. She would be gone for a week. She forwarded all calls to an answering service so their clients would have a way to contact them while they were out of the country. She would allow the receptionist to take her vacation as well at this time. She called Gregg on her way to the car to find out what he wanted for dinner. Before heading home, Kera stopped at the supermarket to pick up a few groceries.

Kera quietly prepared dinner that evening, wanting to make something special for Gregg. This would be the first time they would be away from each other since they became husband and wife. With both of them having such busy schedules, the distance between them wouldn't be as bad.

Gregg watched from the doorway of the kitchen as she prepared their dinner, and a big smile came across his face. "You know, Mrs. Wilson, I'm going to have to give you something to remember me by while we're apart." She turned to see her husband slowly coming towards her with a bouquet of yellow tulips in his hands. Kera knew just what he was thinking, and it made her feel desired.

"Would you help me set the table, please? Dinner will be ready in five minutes," she said.

"I can wait for dinner. Right now, my eyes are set on dessert."

"Now, you know dessert will spoil your appetite?" She looked at him with glossy eyes. She took a deep breath and swallowed hard as he reached out for her.

"I don't care. Besides, I'm so hungry, I could eat the rest afterward." He picked her up, and she wrapped her legs around his waist while kissing him deeply. She dropped the spoon on the counter, and he reached to turn the stove off. Then he took her to the bedroom and made love to her. As the night went on, they totally forgot about dinner.

***

The next morning, Kera got up to finish packing. She made a quick call to Sharon to let her know what time her flight would land. Gregg came into the closet. He hadn't let her out of his sight for long since dinner. She knew he would miss her just as much as she missed him while she was gone.

"I'm meeting Bradley after I take you to the airport so we can go to the gym to work out. You know, I think he's finally getting Sharon out of his system, honey."

"Why? Did he say anything to you?" asked Kera.

"No, I just haven't heard him say anything about her lately. As a matter of fact, he said he received something in the mail regarding the paternity results. I'm not sure what they are, but I'm sure he'll tell me when we get together."

"Okay," said Kera. "You have to call me as soon as you find out. I need to let my girl know what's going on," said Kera.

"Now look, baby, whatever the results are, he has to be the one to tell her. This is their relationship," encouraged Gregg.

"I hear what you're saying, honey, but Sharon is my sister, and I won't leave her in the dark about anything. I don't believe that's right. Don't you think she deserves to know after all she's been through?"

"Yes, but it's still not our business to share. Let him be the one to tell her, not us. He can tell her when you guys fly back into the States. As a matter of fact, I'll wait until you get back to tell you, so you won't spill the news."

She walked over to her husband, kissed him, then turned and pressed her back up against his body. He grabbed her waist and pulled her so tightly, she felt him stiffen against her back. She whispered softly, "If you do that to me, honey, I'll have to put you in timeout for a day. I'm sure you don't want that, do you?" Kera smiled.

He turned her around and said, "There's no way you'll be able to do that. Do you know how I know? I know because we're magnetized to each other. Just being in the same room with me, you won't be able to resist," he said slowly, nibbling on her earlobe. "So don't try to hold back those sweet cookies from me; it won't work. I'm your husband. I need you, just as much as you need me." He kissed her gently and tapped her on her butt as a reminder of what she would be missing out on if she put him on punishment. Her idea of withholding her loving would only make giving in that much sweeter.

She looked at him in a daze and replied, "You know you're wrong for that. I still want to know what the results are. I'll have something for you when I get back." He knew exactly what she meant, and he couldn't wait for her to return to him. The thought of waking up to an empty bed was brutal. Especially when he wanted his wife even more now than when they were just dating.

"I know you will." Smiling as he picked up her suitcases and carried them down the stairs. Gregg knew deep down that this would be hard for both of them to be apart from each other, even for a few days. He would have to occupy his time with something to keep his mind off being away from Kera. Gregg knew the only way he could remain sane was to immerse himself in his work. That was plenty enough by itself. More importantly, he would need to stay around positive people, so that the distance wouldn't become too much for him.

Chapter Twenty-Three

On the way to the airport, Kcra asked Gregg if he would check on her parents and Aunt Patsi for her while she was gone. She also made a laundry list of things to do around the house. Being a wife was surely setting in with her, and the team they created together was everything he'd wanted and more.

He agreed and assured her she didn't have to worry. Gregg gave his wife a big hug and kiss before she went through the checkpoint. He waved to her as she disappeared into the airport terminal.

Once Kera's plane took off, Gregg drove his car straight to Bradley's. He was on edge and could hardly wait to see him. He was concerned for his friend. He also wanted to find out the results of the paternity test.

As he drove up to the ranch, Gregg observed that things seemed a bit still, as if a storm had just blown over. He got out of his car and rang the doorbell. Ken came to the door to let him in. They shook hands, and he showed Gregg into the kitchen where his brothers and their detective friend had gathered.

"What's going on? Why is everyone looking so down?" asked Gregg.

"I received the results today," Bradley said. He handed the letter to Gregg for him to read.

"What does this mean?" Gregg asked after reading the document twice. "I don't understand."

"It means that the test is inconclusive, and they aren't able to make a determination as to whether Bradley is the father," said Charles. "Another test would have to be administered, but the results for this one will only take a day or two. I'm setting up an appointment right now."

"Well, I waited this long; another day or two won't matter." Bradley laughed ruefully.

"So, what's up with the newlyweds? It must be a big change for you now that you've left bachelorhood to the rest of us," Ken said, obviously wanting to lighten the mood in the room.

"I'm glad you asked," Gregg replied. "Man, married life is worth it. I couldn't be a happier man. When you find that woman who completes everything about you, it makes you want to settle down. I love everything about being married. The freedom to express your love in ways you can only imagine as a single person makes me grateful just to have found her."

"I hear you, man. I hear you. One day, I'll find my true love and become a member of the marriage club," replied Ken. The expression on his face was unfamiliar to those in the room. For a moment, Ken showed a real interest in the possibility of tying the knot.

They all looked at each other, sharing a smile, and laughed at the remark made by the youngest in the group, each of them knowing that it would take a miracle for this one to settle down.

"What, you think a brother can't settle down and get married? Oh, what little faith you all have in me. I can't believe this. I bet you that I'll be the first if not the second DuPont brother to get married," said Ken.

"I'd like to see that," said Charles "You'd have to first find a woman who's willing to put up with those spoiled ways of yours. Face it, little brother; you haven't been successful at picking a suitable mate since little Kasey in the ninth grade."

"That's cold. I know. I know. While you're playing, I do wonder what ever became of her."

"Well, if you want, I can look into that for you," said the detective. "I wouldn't even charge you. I like to see men find happiness in his life with the one they love. It would be my pleasure."

"I just may have to take you up on that offer. Her inner beauty was just as beautiful as her outside. I can only imagine it has enhanced even more over the years." He went quiet after that and so did the room.

"Let me know if I can be of assistance. In the meantime, I have to run. I have a long drive ahead of me, then dinner with my wife. Charles, I'll talk to you later."

"Thanks, man. I'll walk you out to your car." Once outside, Charles thanked his friend for all his help. He was humbled at the fact that he was available to help his brothers when they needed him. Eventually, the time would come for him to leave and head back to North Carolina. He had his own affairs to take care of back in Raleigh. Being the eldest of the three, right now, his main concern was making sure his siblings were all right before he left. His heart's desire was to keep the lines of communication open and for them to stay in touch. Charles headed back into the house.

Bradley had gone into the bedroom to get his gym bag. When he came out, he stopped by the living room and picked up his keys from the hall table. Turning to Gregg, Bradley saw that he gained a few pounds while on his honeymoon.

"Are you ready to get those old muscles of yours in shape? Seeing as it looks like you need to work double time to build them up again." Bradley laughed.

"What are you talking about? I'm in the best shape of my life. Ask my wife." Gregg laughed.

"I don't have to ask her. She knows the truth. Let's go before you sprain a muscle walking to the car. We'll see who's in the best shape."

"You done said it. It's on now."

They left the house and headed to the gym. While they were gone, Charles was able to get Bradley an appointment first thing the next morning. He couldn't wait to tell his brother the news. He tried calling him but only reached his voicemail. He and Ken had high hopes that their brother would get through this. He tried to stay positive, so that no matter the outcome of the test, Bradley would know that they would be there to support him.

Gregg couldn't resist asking Bradley about Sharon. He figured this was the perfect time to bring her up, while they were working off some stress. Gregg knew his friend better than anyone, and he felt that he would be honest about his feelings towards her. Bradley and Gregg engaged in intense workouts together each week, which they made into a competition between them. At the end, they would take the usual stroll around the inside track. After their workout, talking seemed to help pass the time as they cooled down from exercising.

"I haven't spoken to her in weeks now. I tried reaching out to her several times, but she never responded. I figured since I haven't gotten a response from her, she doesn't want me anymore. So, as a result, I've decided to give her space and possibly let her go."

"I find that hard to believe. That's not the Bradley I know. Sounds like you're giving up on you two. If that's the case, you should never give up hope. You two are going through a rough patch in your relationship, but that doesn't mean it isn't meant to be. If you give up when things get tough, that means you didn't want it as much as you say you do. If you continue fighting for it, then it makes it worth the fight," said Gregg.

"Yeah, I hear what you're saying, but I feel like I'm fighting by myself. It's torture for me. It torments my soul. I don't want to think about being without her, but I don't want to feel like I'm fighting for someone who doesn't want me. Do I think about her? Yes! Do I still want to have her in my life? Every day, I want her with me, but those are *my* wants. She has to want me also."

"You're right. I just hate to see you go through so much pain knowing that you want to be with her. I only want to see you happy, and I know that if it's meant to be, it will work out. Just don't be so quick to let it go without seeing where it will lead."

"Thanks, man. I appreciate your concern. I've just accepted the fact that we may never be together. That's not the same as giving up. She left me without hearing what I had to say, and that hurt me. After all we've experienced together, it seemed like it was easy for her to just leave like that. It stings deep."

He turned his head to hide the tears welling up in his eyes. Gregg felt the pain his friend felt and decided to lighten things up a bit.

"Okay. Let's grab a bite to eat. I'm starving, and you look like you need some nourishment." Bradley smiled slightly, just enough for his spirit to lift from the heaviness he felt. They walked into the locker room to shower and change clothes. As they headed out of the gym, Bradley pulled his cell phone out of his gym bag and listened to his messages. He heard the voicemail his brother left about the test tomorrow. He gave a deep sigh and said, "Round two begins!"

"What do you mean round two? What's that about?" Gregg asked. He'd only hope that it was better news than what Bradley showed on his face.

"Charles left a message that I'm scheduled to take the test again tomorrow morning. He said Catherine will be there with her son, so we can both test at the same time."

"You have to keep the faith. This too shall pass, and you'll be able to put this behind you. Anyway, it's best you get this over with now rather than later."

"I hope you're right, my friend. I hope you're right. I feel like I'm on a roller coaster, and the ride isn't at a stopping point for me to get off. I'm just tired," replied Bradley.

"Hey, it's all going to work out. You'll see. I know you're tired. Speaking of tired, I need some energy myself. Besides, I can't think of anything I'd rather do right now than to find somewhere to fill up my stomach." Gregg laughed. "Where do you want to eat?"

"Let's go someplace where we can get a good salad or something light to eat. I don't want to put just anything in my body after working out. Eating the wrong thing and too much of the wrong thing will defeat the purpose of exercising," said Bradley.

"I agree. Let's go to that place downtown."

"Okay, cool. Lead the way." They both got in their cars and headed to one of their favorite restaurants off Gervais Street. It was a beautiful day, and traffic was unusually light going into downtown Columbia around noon. They reached their destination in record time by fifteen minutes, escaping through every traffic light before turning red.

As the hour passed, they finished their lunch and parted ways for the day. Gregg made a stop at the in-laws' house to check on them first. Instead of driving to Aunt Patsi's house, he decided to call her, but she didn't answer her phone.

**

Bradley got up early to take a jog around the ranch before heading out to the clinic. He enjoyed running and breathing in nature's air first thing in the morning. Nothing could compare to the peace he felt, except the thought of waking up next to Sharon. He stopped short of reaching the house to catch his breath.

Standing by the pond on their ranch, he watched the ducks swimming as though they were without a care in the world. Oh, to be like one of them, he thought. Part of him wanted to scream out as if he were in agony, but the other part wouldn't let him. He came from a line of strong men, who always knew how to handle themselves in any situation. The challenges he faced in the past were nothing compared to what he was going through. He thought losing his parents and grandparents was hard, but losing Sharon was even harder for him to handle.

Chapter Twenty-Four

Sharon waited at the Paris airport for Kera to arrive. Both excited and anxious, she stood with her back turned away from the crowd. All of a sudden, a voice rang out to her. She turned to face her friend, knowing fully it was Kera. She looked amazing. Sharon reached out to hug her, and the next thing she knew, they were jumping up and down, ignorant of people's stares as they passed by. The two friends were so excited to see each other, they didn't take notice of anyone else at the airport.

"Oh, my goodness, girl," said Kera. "Paris is so beautiful. Well, at least what I saw of it as I flew in. I'm so excited to be here. You look amazing. Paris looks good on you. How are you?"

"I'm good. I was going to call you, but I wanted to wait until you got here for us to catch up. I've missed you a lot." Sharon hugged her friend tightly, and immediately she knew something was going on with her.

Kera felt deep inside that Sharon's last reaction told of her somber mood, and it had to do with Bradley. Her gut instinct told her that she needed to find out.

"Is everything all right with you, sis?"

"Yes, it will be. I missed you a lot, that's all. We have so much to catch up on and so much to see. Come, let's go to the hotel and get you settled in."

On the way to the hotel, Sharon shared information about a few sites they passed. Some of the apprehension Kera felt in the airport ebbed as they talked in the car.

Sharon ordered lunch while Kera unpacked her luggage. When she was finished, she came into the living room and sat by her friend. The air felt so thick again around Sharon, she didn't know what to say without ending up burying her face in tears.

"What's going on with you, girl?" asked Kera. She retrieved a box of Kleenex from the coffee table.

"I'm in a terrible situation, Kera, and I don't know what to do," cried Sharon. The tears streamed down her face, and she was unable to stop crying. Kera reached out her arms to hold Sharon.

"There! There! Sis! Tell me what's got you so upset. Or can I take a guess?" asked Kera.

"It's not what you think. Well, it is sort of. Kera, I found out I'm about six weeks pregnant, and I don't know what to do. This isn't how I planned my life. I was supposed to have my career, get married, and then have children. This is far from it."

"Wow! That far long? I'm so sorry you felt you had to carry this burden alone. Honey, you should have called me. How did you find out?"

"One evening after work, a group of us got together for dinner. I had been tired for about a week, and I thought it was because of working so much, or maybe it was the change in the weather and location. Anyway, I got really sick and passed out in the restaurant bathroom of all places. They rushed me to the hospital so quickly, I didn't know what was happening. The doctor did some test, but they weren't sure of the reason I was sick."

"So, how did they come to the conclusion you were pregnant if the test weren't showing anything?"

"The first test showed I was dehydrated. When they did a urinalysis, it came back negative, but the doctor said he wanted to get some blood work on me. So, they did. When the blood work came back, they had the answer."

Kera turned sideways on the sofa to face Sharon. "You're pregnant. That's a good thing! It means I'm going to be an auntie! We have to celebrate!" She glanced off to the side for a second, imagining all the things she would buy for the baby.

"How can you be so excited? This is a messed-up situation," cried Sharon.

"What do you mean messed up? God don't make messes. He blesses! Recognize, honey, that this is a blessing. You of all people should know this. This baby will be loved by everyone in his or her life. You need to understand that."

"To be honest, it's hard for me to see too much good about this situation right now. I was intent on working on myself, and I was making headway. It wasn't for nothing, but this is a hurdle I never expected to have to clear. I don't want to be alone. I don't want to raise this baby alone. I can't see myself taking care of a fragile life on my own."

"Please tell me you've told Bradley," Kera asked.

"No, and I don't think I'm going to. At least not right now. I mean he's already going through paternity testing with Catherine. I don't want to add more pressure or responsibilities on him. Two children by two different women is a lot for anyone to deal with."

"Don't you see he doesn't care about her? I'm sure if the test result says he's the father of her child, he'll do the right thing by taking care of him but have as little contact with her as possible. You, on the other hand, are the woman he loves, and he would be in both of your lives. Everyone knew by looking at you two at our wedding that you two were made for each other." Kera drew in a deep breath and focused her gaze directly on Sharon.

"The way he looks at you. The way your eyes light up when you two are together. This baby would bring so much happiness to your lives. I'm excited and happy for you both. You won't be able to hide this from him for too long. You have to tell him so he can be here for you and the baby. So, snap out of it. Be the big girl that you are and tell the man."

"Okay, I'll tell him when we get back to the States on Thursday."

They continued talking until late into the night. They talked about everything from the success of the business to their visions for their personal lives. It was like they were two middle school girls, talking about a future life—except they were already living it.

The next morning would be a full day at the office. With meeting after meeting, they would hardly have time to talk during the day. They looked forward to quitting time so they could unwind and relax.

***

Bradley mentally prepared himself for the second paternity test. He was about to leave the house for the clinic when his phone rang.

"Hello?"

"Mr. Bradley DuPont?"

"Yes?"

"This is Nurse Jackson."

"Ah. Yes. I was just about to be on my way."

"Yes. That's why I'm calling."

Bradley paused at his car. "Okay."

"It looks like there was a bit of a mix up with the administrative work."

Bradley's stomach bottomed out. He couldn't take another delay. "Please don't tell me I can't get tested today."

"No. Well. Yes. I'm saying, rather poorly, that you don't need to come in to get retested. The paperwork somehow got switched. Your results from your first test showed that you couldn't be the other subject's father."

Bradley slid down the side of his car to land on his butt. He was both stunned and dazed. It was over. He was free. He was finally free.

"Will you relay the results to the other party?"

"Yes. They're next on my list. I sincerely apologize for the confusion. We take full responsibility for the mix-up in the results you were provided. I assure you this has never happened before and there's no excuse for it."

"Ma'am, there's no need for an apology. I appreciate you calling and letting me know. You don't know how much this means to me. Thank you so much," Bradley said with a sigh.

"Well, I have your results here on my desk, but I'm leaving the office in about an hour and a half. If you would like, you can stop by and pick them up before I leave."

Bradley immediately responded, "I'll be there before you leave! I'm on my way now. Thanks again."

Bradley hung the phone up and ran back into the house to tell his brothers the news.

"There's no way I'm letting you go alone. In fact, I'll drive," Charles said.

"I'm going too. You're not leaving me out of this," Ken piped in. The three of them got in Bradley's car and headed to the clinic.

Bradley could feel in his bones that this was a new start for him. There was only one problem. The one person he wanted to share the news with was thousands of miles away, and he wasn't sure how she would react.

Traffic was heavy, and Bradley was afraid they wouldn't make it in time. He wanted that paperwork in his hand so he could give it to Charles today. He wanted it legally served to Catherine as quickly as possible to get her out of his hair.

Just as they pulled in the parking lot, he spotted a woman walking out of the building and heading towards a parked Mercedes GLE Coupe. She was casually dressed in a pair of fitted slacks, a short-sleeved, half-buttoned blouse, and flat shoes.

Bradley pointed to the woman in case his brothers missed her. "That must be Nurse Jackson. We made it just in time." Charles pulled up beside her and threw the car into park.

"Hi, Nurse Jackson?"

She nodded.

"I'm Bradley DuPont. I met you for my first test. I'm sorry for being late," he told her. "Traffic was horrible on the 20."

"It's no problem. I actually just came out here to put some things in my car. Let's go back in to get you your paperwork. Again, I'm sorry for the mix-up. This is the first time this has happened in my fifteen years as a nurse practitioner."

Bradley took a couple of steps before he remembered his brothers.

"Let me introduce you to my brothers. They were my rocks throughout this entire nightmare." He signaled for them to follow. Both Charles and Ken got out to greet the young nurse.

When Ken got out of the car, he stopped in his tracks with his mouth wide open. His expression was that of a deer caught staring in the headlights of an on-coming vehicle.

"Oh, my goodness, I can't believe it! Kasey Jackson, is that you?" he asked. "Dang, life has been good to you."

"Why, Ken DuPont, I haven't seen you since... high school. What a coincidence!"

Both Bradley and Charles moved to the side, watching the two of them get reacquainted.

Charles gave his brother a nudge on his arm. "That's little Kacey Jackson all grown up. She's the one they were teasing him about."

Bradley glanced at him, then the woman again. "What a small world."

"Looks like you don't need that detective after all." Charles laughed. Ken gave him a stare so he would shut up.

"Kasey, I don't know if you remember my brothers, though I think you've already met them—Charles and Bradley."

"It's nice to see you both again. You know, I looked at the last name when you came to the clinic for your appointment, and I wanted to ask if there was any relation between the two of you. I was so busy that I forgot. It's amazing. I've been wondering what happened to you. A while back, I even asked your cousin Ben if he'd seen you lately. How have you been?"

"I've been good. You know, this is really strange. I was just talking about you the other day, and here you are. I always knew you would turn out to be a beautiful woman even when we were kids. I'm glad I'm able to see it with my own eyes."

"Yeah, he was going to find you. You can believe that," mumbled Charles.

"He was even going to pay to find you," mumbled Bradley. The two of them laughed and followed Ms. Jackson and Ken back into the clinic so Bradley could get his paperwork.

"I'd like to call you some time if that's all right with you?" asked Ken.

"I would like that very much."

Ken pulled out his phone so that he could put her number in his contact list.

"That sounds great! I guess I should have asked if you're seeing someone first. I don't want to step on anybody's toes. Not that it would bother me at all."

"I see that you haven't changed much. You're just as cocky now as you were back then." Her lips lifted into a smile, which revealed the dimples hidden within her smooth cheeks. Her beautiful dark complexion was so radiant, he couldn't take his eyes off her.

"Hey, I don't back down from pursuing something I want. Right now, I see all that I want to pursue in front of me."

"We'll see just how much you want to pursue me. I anticipate that call."

"You'll get it," he responded with a grin. Then she surprised all of them by stepping into her space and giving her a hug. "It's good to see you again, Kasey." He let her go but steadied her until she looked more stable on her own feet.

"I'll call you later this week, so we can set a date for dinner," he said as they walked her back to her car.

"I look forward to it." She smiled as she got in her car.

Ken watched as she drove away. Then he headed back to Bradley's car, noticing that his brothers were watching the entire time. Once inside, he didn't say a word. Bradley and Charles burst into laughter. Ken knew he would have to hear his brother's jokes the entire ride.

"I have to hand it to you, little brother. That was a smooth move. We saw how she went limp on you." Bradley laughed.

"I'm sure her body doesn't know what to think right now," said Charles. "She probably had to pull over somewhere to get her thoughts together. It wouldn't surprise me one bit, being that we seem to have taught you very well."

"Okay, you both have had your fun. Let's go already," exclaimed Ken. "But you're right. She has always held a special place in my heart. There was no other girl in school that could keep me in my place but still treated me with respect. I'm going to give it my all to make this work," said Ken.

Chapter Twenty-Five

THEY ALL MET UP with Gregg at the local sports bar to celebrate the good news about Bradley's paternity test. They even talked about Ken's reunion with his long-lost love. They couldn't help joking around with him. Everyone was having a good time.

"I guess you're next, Charles," said Gregg.

"I'm good. I'll leave the love thing to you all. I'm up to my eyelids in cases. I can't see anything but paperwork."

"It has to be someone that you're interested in," said Ken.

"Nope, not really, man. Most workaholics don't have the pleasure of dating."

"All work and no play make Charles an old man," said Gregg. "By the time you get a woman, she'll have to teach you some things." They all laughed at him.

"Don't let this workaholic fool you," said Charles. "I still know how to get a woman. Getting a woman isn't a top priority right now."

It was getting dark, and Gregg had to make sure he was home in time to FaceTime Kera. That was their nightly thing to do since they were in different time zones. He couldn't wait to see her beautiful face.

"Well, fellas," Gregg said, "it's time for me to bid you farewell. I have a very important meeting to attend. You'll all have to carry on without me."

"What kind of meeting are you attending?" asked Ken.

"You're too nosey. If you must know, it's the wife, and I'm not fooling around with you three and messing up my happy home. On that note, good night, gentlemen."

"All right, man. I don't blame you one bit," said Bradley. "Talk with you later," said Bradley.

Before Gregg got in his car, he turned to face Bradley and said, "Hey, man. If you want, I'll ask Kera how Sharon is doing and give you an update."

"It's okay. Spend that time with your wife. If Sharon wants to talk to me, my number hasn't changed."

"You two are the most stubborn people I know, but it's totally up to you." Gregg got in his car and drove away. Not long afterward, the brothers piled into Bradley's car and headed home also.

***

Three days had passed since Bradley had spoken to Gregg. He wondered how he was doing and decided to give him a quick call to check on him. Before he could dial the number, Gregg called on his phone.

"Hey, man. What's up with you?" Gregg told him that Kera had gotten some tickets for him to go to the soccer tournament and wanted him to come up for two days. The investors had given her and Sharon four complimentary tickets. He told him that Sharon was feeling well, but he thought she could use some company. It took a lot to convince Bradley to even go with him, but it worked out in the end.

A lot of time had passed between Sharon and Bradley's last encounter. He felt that rekindling their love became a thing of the past. Still, he couldn't get her out of his mind, although each day, it was getting a little better.

He needed to see her face to face to find out if they could make their relationship work. If not, he would swallow his pride and come back home with at least some closure. The past few months had been torturous, and he needed to release the tension he felt.

Bradley wasted no time getting ready for the journey. He ran into his room and packed a bag. Charles peeked into his room to find out what was going on. Bradley moved so fast to get out of the house, he barely noticed his brother talking to him. Ken heard the commotion, and he also peeked in to find out what was happening.

"I don't have much time to explain," Bradley said. "I'm going out of town for a few days, and I have a plane to catch in three hours." He stood still for a second and felt hope stemming from deep inside.

He turned to his brothers and said, "Sharon needs me, so I'm going to Paris to make sure she's all right. I love her, so I'm going to get my woman back."

Charles and Ken looked at each other and applauded. They were so excited for their brother, they helped him pack his suitcase.

"We got you covered, man," said Ken. "Go get her."

"Thanks, man. I love you guys. I'll call you when I get there."

***

Bradley and Gregg arrived at the airport and unloaded their luggage. Gregg saw his friend's hands shaking. He told him that everything would be all right. Trying to build up his nerves, he decided to think positive. He convinced himself of two things. She would either welcome him into her heart, or he would return to the States without his love by his side.

Kera and Sharon left for the office for their meeting. The aroma of fresh-baked pastries from a nearby bakery filled almost every corner. Once the cab reached the building, they stopped at a nearby park and decided to walk the rest of the way. Sharon showed Kera the beautiful sculptures and the cathedral that had the appearance of something heavenly. Kera stood in awe as she gazed upon the scenery.

The day ended, and the two of them grabbed dinner at one of the restaurants before heading back to the apartment. The meeting had been very successful, and they were very pleased with the way God planned their lives. They sat on the hotel room sofa, ready to relax and watch a movie, when there was a knock at the door.

"Were you expecting any company?" Kera asked.

"No... I'm not expecting anyone. It could be the doorman bringing the mail. Would you answer it while I get us something to drink, please?"

Kera went to the door to see who it was. She looked through the peephole, and immediately, a smile came across her face. It was Gregg. She opened the door and stepped back to let him in. After giving him a hug and a kiss, she looked back and noticed someone with him. Just then, Sharon came around the corner and saw Bradley.

Sharon couldn't believe her eyes. She stood, frozen, not knowing what to do. Part of her wanted to walk into her room and hide. The other part wanted to run to the man she loved.

Kera and Gregg saw what was happening between the two of them. Holding each other tightly, Gregg decided to break the tension in the room and greeted Sharon with a hello. She responded but couldn't take her eyes off Bradley. It was as though a block of cement held her in place so she wouldn't move. She felt uncomfortable in her oversized t-shirt and house socks.

Kera explained to Gregg that they weren't expecting them, and they were just about to sit to watch a movie. Sharon finally got the courage to say something, but she didn't know what she wanted to say. This was the moment she had dreaded yet anticipated.

"Bradley... What are you doing here?" she asked. "How did you find me?"

He walked over to her and gazed into eyes. She felt her defenses were no match for him. He was a man she couldn't resist. He was a man she didn't want to resist.

"I had to come and see how you were doing," he said. He attempted to reach out and touch her, but she quickly stepped back. He felt his heart drop with a thump. His fears of having lost her were coming forward again, and he didn't know how to respond.

This won't be easy. I have to make this right, or I may never get another chance.

"You didn't have to come," she said. Sharon walked past him to sit on the sofa, trying hard not to stare. She wasn't prepared for the conversation she needed to have with him. She attempted to give him the cold shoulder as if she were still upset. She wasn't sure how long she could keep up that appearance.

"Yes, I did have to come. I tried calling you. I left a bunch of mes-sages, but you never responded to any of them. So, you see, I needed to come. I want to be here." He followed her into the living room and sat beside her. It took every fiber in him not to touch her. He placed his hands on his lap and put his hands together so he could have control over them.

"You don't have to worry about me. I'm a big girl, and I'm surely capable of taking care of myself. You need to be concerned about you and…" Kera cleared her throat so Sharon would be careful about what her next words would be.

Bradley glanced over at his friends and said, "I'm sorry, you guys."

"It's okay. Don't mind us. You two go ahead and talk; we'll be in the other room." They disappeared into the hall. Kera couldn't help how happy she felt for Sharon and Bradley to finally be in the same room after so much time spent apart.

Chapter Twenty-Six

BRADLEY NOTICED SOMETHING DIFFERENT about Sharon. Her eyes told him that she was keeping something from him. Every time he looked at her, she would find something else to focus on. Even though she wore an oversized shirt which hid her figure—or so she thought—wasn't doing much. He could still remember what she looked like without having anything on.

She stood in front of the sofa and was about to say something to him. He stood beside her. Sitting so close to her without being able to touch her was agonizing. He couldn't control his hands any longer. He had been waiting and fantasizing for a long time to hold her again. His chest touched her forehead. The smell of her freshly washed hair sent signals to his lower extremities. He then ran his fingers through her hair and caressed the back of her neck.

As he held her, he took one hand and ran it over the side of her body. He felt the difference in her waist and couldn't help gliding his fingers over her abdomen. He leaned back, still holding her tightly, and looked into her almond-shaped eyes. He pulled her close to him and kissed her passionately.

All she could do at this point was participate and give in to his advances. She couldn't resist anymore. She already felt the effects of the pregnancy and putting up a fight wasn't an option. She was happy he was there. She needed him like never before. Still wrapped in his arms, she continued kissing him. At least until she felt so nauseated, she promptly broke free from him to run to the bathroom.

In that room, her secret revealed itself. All she could think about was how he would react to finding out the cause of her nausea. Fear and sickness came over her like a speeding train. She tried to close the door behind her so he wouldn't see her, but it was too late.

From the bathroom doorway, Bradley saw her on her knees, throwing up. It seemed violent, and it scared him, as he didn't know what was causing her to be sick. A sense of worry crept in and crowded his thoughts. Bradley pushed the bathroom door open to reveal a weakened Sharon crouched on the floor. She held onto the toilet as if she were on a cliff about to fall over.

"Sharon, are you all right? What can I do?" he asked.

Bradley wanted to rush in and save her from all she was going through. The adrenaline running through his body made him want to swoop her up and hold her until she felt better. He wanted her to know he was there for her. She turned slightly, and, with a despondent expression, she relaxed her head on the toilet bowl.

"Nothing, now please go away! I'm all right."

He knew she was embarrassed to be seen that way, but there was no way he wouldn't help her through this.

"That's not true," said Bradley. "I can see that you're not feeling well. Here, let me help you."

He grabbed a face towel from the rack and wet it with cold water. He walked over to her and found her face was still buried in the toilet. He placed the cool towel over her neck and massaged her back to help soothe her.

"I'm here, honey, and I'm not leaving you like this. Please don't shut me out. Should I call for a doctor?"

"No, there's no need for that. I'll be better once I lie down. Besides, I'm getting used to this." Bradley helped her get up from the floor. She stumbled over to the sink to wash her face and brush her teeth. He walked out of the bathroom and sat on the bed. He had heard what she said but wanted to find out what she meant.

As he waited for her to come out, his mind raced with frightening thoughts. Did she have some serious illness he wasn't aware of that required medical attention? He didn't know what to think, or whether he would even understand once she'd told him. He tried to prepare himself for what may be the inevitable. Still, he tried not to think of the worst.

Sharon came out of the bathroom, too weak to stand. He helped her onto the bed and pulled a blanket over her. She looked at him with an unusual look of concern. Taking in a deep breath, she closed her eyes and reached her hand out to hold his.

After watching him take care of her, she knew she couldn't hold off telling him that he would be a father to their unborn child. Opening her eyes, she gave him a smile, and it belayed some of his fears. She propped herself up on the pillows before speaking.

"Bradley, I need to tell you something, and I admit I've been fearful considering the recent events that have taken place between us."

"What is it, baby? You don't ever have to be afraid to talk to me. I'll do everything in my power to make sure you're taken care of. No matter how serious the situation may be."

"I don't quite know how to say this. I wanted to tell you the minute I found out, but I was too scared."

"I'm here, and like I said earlier, I'm not going anywhere," he said. He could tell that whatever it was she was about to tell him was very hard for her. He gave her a smile to ease her fears. Suddenly, tears streamed down her face. He reached up to wipe them away. He leaned in closer to her so she could feel safe when she was with him.

She placed his hand on her stomach. After taking in a few deep breaths, she looked back up at him. "We're going to have a baby."

Bradley stood. All he could do was watch her. He didn't say anything for several minutes. His body signals were all over the place as he took it all in.

"I don't know what to say," he said. "I'm at a loss for words right now. I mean... I'm astonished to hear this news. How long have you known?"

She stared up at him for a moment. Her eyes roved around his face. Then she drew in a ragged breath. "You don't have to say anything. I'll take care of the baby on my own. I know that having two children will be a lot for you to handle."

His heart sank when he considered her words and realized he had given her the wrong impression. He leaned over, pulled her close to him, and kissed her.

"No, baby, you don't understand. I'm in shock. You've just made me the happiest man in the world. We'll take care of our baby together. I want you, and I want our baby. I hope it's not too late for us. I love you, Sharon, and nothing will ever change that.

"I haven't felt this way about any other woman in my life. There's no one else I would rather have my children with than you. I'm all yours. Please say you'll have me."

Sharon cried tears of relief. He reached down once again and kissed her. When the tears subsided a little, she asked, "What about your son with Catherine?"

"We were tested, and her child isn't my son. Charles is taking care of all of the legalities behind her trying to get money from yet another man for her child." He waited for her response but once a few seconds passed, and she didn't say anything, he went on.

"My house is clean and waiting for you." They had both spent too much time trying to piece together a relationship that should never have been pulled a part. He was ready to move on to the happy ending they had both been hoping for.

Sharon decided that enough pain had been inflicted by the selfishness and stupidity of a vindictive person. There was no need for her to harbor ill feelings towards Catherine. She knew it wouldn't be right. In a crazy way, she actually felt sorry for the woman. Besides, she had to deal with her own issues of trust, belief, and self-love.

"When I got the news about the paternity test, I wanted to catch the first flight out of the States. I wanted so desperately to share it with you." As he spoke, he stretched out beside her. Studying his body language, she could tell he was up to something. Her heart pounded rapidly in her chest. Anxiety set in deeper with every breath she took. He took her hand, reached into his pocket, and held up one of the biggest diamonds she had ever seen. She couldn't help the gasp that came from her lips.

"Sharon Gable, will you do me the honor of and making my life complete by becoming my wife? You're the only woman I want to spend the rest of my life with."

"Yes, Bradley. I would love to be your wife." He pushed the ring on her finger. She gently pulled his face towards hers and kissed him. A tear of happiness ran down his face. She leaned in to kiss the tear away, letting him know she was his, and he was hers.

***

"It's about time. Now I can help plan your wedding," cried Kera. Bradley looked at her, wondering how much of their intimate conversation she'd witnessed.

"I wasn't spying. Honest. I wanted to check on you guys, and I just happened to see him proposing. I was praying that you two would stop playing around and get back together. It all worked out according to God's timing and plan. Gregg and I knew that you two were made for each other from the first time you met. Imagine the four of us here in this beautiful country. You know Paris is known as the city of love? Congratulations, family. And on that note, I'm going to say good night!"

Kera and Gregg walked back into the bedroom. Gregg was exhausted from the flight and the long drive to the hotel. He undressed to take a shower and once he stepped under the warm water, his body felt relaxed. He hadn't been in the shower for more than five minutes. Suddenly, he felt a soft hand glide across his wet skin. The steam from the shower had become steamier once she joined him. He placed his arms around her waist and kissed her from her forehead, and then his lips rested on hers. They weren't concerned about anything or anyone. All they wanted was each other. It had been a few days since she left for Paris, and he wanted to make up for time lost.

"I've missed you, sweetheart," he whispered softly to her. His arms slid across her shoulders, down her chest until he reached her rounded derriere. She moaned in excitement as he rubbed and embraced her. The warm water poured down on them as if it were heavy rain. His hands circulated her entire frame. He sat on the shower seat to make it easier for her to sit on him. This sent messages to her core.

Since they were married, their lovemaking was more powerful. The freedom to express themselves without guilt was in their divine rights. Gregg made sure to concentrate on the parts of her that would give her the most satisfaction. The penetration of their bodies joined together gave them so much pleasure as they reached the climax of their lovemaking. Slowly moving his hips, he wanted to make sure it had a lasting effect in that moment.

Once out of the shower, the yearning to make love to his wife again was ever present on him. He was so in love with her. He couldn't help thinking of how much he wanted to express his desires with her. He carried her to the bed and continued giving himself to her. Romance was definitely in this hotel suite. No one paid attention to the other, for both couples expressed their lustful thirst towards their mate.

***

Bradley looked at his wife-to-be and caressed her abdomen, which held their unborn child. He looked at her as if it were the first time they had laid eyes on each other. While she relaxed on the bed, he massaged her feet. He worked his way up her legs while slowly kissing parts that screamed for him to touch. It wasn't long before their bodies were combined in a heated passion of lovemaking.

Despite the initial challenges that threatened their romance, they were now able to enjoy all their desires. The confirmation of their soon-to-be union heightened the intensity of their lovemaking. This went on for hours throughout the night.

Now that they had resolved most of their past mental and emotional struggles, after the heated lovemaking, the stressful tension from her body soon dissipated, and she fell fast asleep.

Bradley stayed awake a little while after. He thanked God for another chance and that she agreed to be his wife. He thought about how grateful he was to have such a wonderful woman in his life. He felt very appreciative for all that he had gone through. If it hadn't been for those experiences, he wouldn't be the man Gramps instilled in him to be.

He knew that, in this life, to get your heart's desires, you have to be patient with the process. These past weeks without Sharon had surely tested his patience. He vowed to himself that from this day forward, he would keep his faith in love—their love.

A big smile came across his face. Everything Gramps had told him regarding Sharon had come true. He couldn't wait to get back home and share the news with his siblings. He closed his eyes, wrapped his arms around her, and fell into a peaceful sleep.

Chapter Twenty-Seven

THE NEXT MORNING, THE two men were in the kitchen making breakfast for their favorite women in the world.

Kera smelled bacon as the scent of it slipped under the door of her bedroom. She turned over, felt the side of the bed where Gregg had been, and noticed he wasn't there. She opened her eyes and glanced around the room. Immediately, she knew he was the one who had the hotel suite smelling so good.

"There's nothing like the smell of smoked Applewood bacon in the morning," she said to herself. Room service was fantastic. She got up, grabbed her robe, and headed towards the breakfast nook on the balcony off of the living room.

As she approached, she heard the two men laughing and talking, and she decided not to interrupt their male bonding moment. Turning towards Sharon's room, she noticed that her door was still closed. She knocked, but there was no answer.

She knocked again. Still no response from inside the room. She opened the door slightly to see that her friend was still sleeping.

She must have had a pleasurable night.

Seeing that Sharon didn't realize that she had opened the door, Kera tipped in to see if she was okay. Her friend looked so peaceful, she decided not to bother her. As she turned to walk out of the room, she heard movement as Sharon woke up.

"Kera, I know it's you; I can smell your body spray," Sharon said, laughing.

"Girl, I didn't want to wake you. You looked so peaceful sleeping. I just wanted to check in on you."

"I slept like a baby last night. What time is it?"

"It's almost noon," answered Kera.

"Oh great! One more day, and we'll be heading back home. I could stay here forever. This place is wonderful."

"It is, isn't it? But one of us will be here more than the other to make sure our business is successful here as it is at home. Have you told Bradley about the opportunity we have here?"

"We discussed it briefly, but we really didn't do much talking last night." Sharon giggled.

"I bet you didn't. Child, he looked like you were a plate of food when they arrived. I thought we would have to hose him down from wanting to jump your bones to death." They laughed so loud, their voices rang throughout the room.

Sharon looked around and asked, "Is that bacon I smell?"

"It sure is. Our men are in the kitchen cooking breakfast and having a grand ol' time."

"I'm glad we're all here together. I'm especially glad that I have so much support around me."

"That's what sisters are for," said Kera. "Always." She reached over to hug her. Sharon pulled Kera onto the bed, and the two reminisced about their childhood and made plans to show Bradley and Gregg some of the places they had visited in Paris later that afternoon.

In the middle of their conversation, Sharon's phone buzzed with a text message. She looked over to see who it was from. Sharon sat straight up in bed as she read the message.

"What is it?" asked Kera.

"You won't believe this. I know this has to be a mistake."

"What?"

Sharon took her time reading the message again. She shook her head in disbelief. She hadn't seen this one coming at all. She turned to Kera with a serious look on her face. Kera sat up, not knowing what to think of Sharon's reactions. Sharon burst into laughter, and Kera couldn't help taking a peek at the message.

"Say what? How in the world..." Sharon handed the phone to her so she could read the whole thing. As Kera read the message, her eyes stretched wide open. She couldn't hold it in any longer. She too burst into laughter.

"I don't know why we're acting surprised. I mean this *is* Aunt Patsi," said Sharon.

"I knew Aunt Patsi was a freak but not like that. I wonder who she was sending it to."

"Apparently, you didn't read the whole thing!" exclaimed Sharon. "Keep reading."

She read the message in its entirety. Trying hard not to imagine her aunt doing the things she described in the text was nearly impossible.

"I can't... Clinton? Of all men in this world, she picked him. They looked at each other in amazement."

"Well, we both know that she's one woman who doesn't discriminate. It doesn't matter about his age. If he has the spoon to go in her ice cream, then she has no problem with him," said Sharon. They gazed off into the room, trying hard not to imagine Clinton and their aunt together.

Bradley and Gregg entered the room to inform them that breakfast was ready. They noticed the two were preoccupied in thought.

"Is everything all right, honey?" asked Gregg.

"Yes, everything's all right," said Kera. "We were just trying to figure out what sites we wanted to see today."

She glanced over at Sharon as if to say, *this is our little secret*.

***

Sharon remembered the conversations she and Aunt Patsi had prior to her leaving for Paris. She felt somewhat happy yet sympathetic to her. She wondered how she must be feeling. Patsi was still a very attractive woman for her age. You wouldn't have known she was as old as she was; her body was in magnificent shape. She could see why Clinton, or any other man for that matter, would want her.

Sharon sensed that once Aunt Patsi realized she'd sent the message to the wrong person, she would be calling her to explain the mix up. All she could do was to try to prepare for the call.

Kera and Gregg walked to the balcony to eat their breakfast. Bradley stayed behind to make sure Sharon was okay to come out with them. He wanted to make sure she could keep the food in her stomach.

"If you want, I can bring you breakfast in bed," he said.

"No, I want to come and eat breakfast with everyone."

Bradley helped her from the bed and slipped her robe around her. The two of them joined their friends at the table.

As Sharon glanced at her handsome fiancé from across the table, she realized that she had gotten her Boaz after all.

About the Author

M.M. SKYE IS AN entrepreneur and contemporary romance writer. A native of South Carolina, M.M. Skye has a diverse background in education and business. With her passion for storytelling and a love for cultural diversity, M. M. Skye's books offer a unique blend of romance and cultural immersion.

You can find her with a book or a pen and paper somewhere ready to create unique characters and stories the reader can relate to. Her passion for writing began in middle school when she read her first novel. It wasn't until high school when her tenth-grade honors English teacher encouraged her to major in English, that she began weaving tales.

Her time at Voorhees University gave her the extra knowledge she needed to hone her craft. Away with Shadows is her debut novel.

www.ingramcontent.com/pod-product-compliance
Lightning Source LLC
Chambersburg PA
CBHW061259210726
48293CB00003B/1027